■ □ ■ □ ■

LODGERS

■ □ ■ □ ■

NENAD VELIČKOVIĆ

LODGERS

Translated from the Yugoslavian
by Celia Hawkesworth

NORTHWESTERN UNIVERSITY PRESS

EVANSTON, ILLINOIS

Northwestern University Press
Evanston, Illinois 60208-4170

Copyright © 2005 by Northwestern University Press.
Published 2005 by Northwestern University Press. All rights reserved.

Printed in the United States of America

10 9 8 7 6 5 4 3 2 1

ISBN 0-8101-2241-3 (cloth)
ISBN 0-8101-2242-1 (paper)

"Yugoslavian" is the author's preferred term for the language previously known as
Serbo-Croatian (now called Bosnian, Croatian, or Serbian).

Library of Congress Cataloging-in-Publication Data

Veličković, Nenad, 1962–
  [Konačari. English]
  Lodgers / Nenad Velickovic ; translated by Celia Hawkesworth.
     p.   cm. — (Writings from an unbound Europe)
  ISBN 0-8101-2241-3 (cloth : alk. paper) — ISBN 0-8101-2242-1 (pbk. : alk. paper)
  1. Hawkesworth, Celia, 1942– . II. Title. III. Series.
PG1619.32.E42K6613 2005
891.8′236—dc22

                                                                    2005001657

♾ The paper used in this publication meets the minimum requirements of the American
National Standard for Information Sciences—Permanence of Paper for Printed Library
Materials, ANSI z39.48-1992.

■ □ ■ □ ■

LODGERS

■ □ ■ □ ■

The apple tree in front of Alma's window had been severed by shrapnel. Some branches still hung from thin yellow belts of bark, others had sprinkled the earth round the tree and pieces of the sparrows' broken birdhouse with pale pink blossom. Only one shell had fallen, and only one piece of shrapnel hit Alma. Some flowers were wilting, scorched by drops of already blackened blood. In Turkish, Alma means apple.

We were sitting in the museum, silent over our undrunk coffee, waiting for news from the hospital, and we didn't know whether we were more afraid or ashamed. Alma had great plans for this spring: she was supposed to fall in love, to write her first poem, to play in a public concert. I was ashamed, because I didn't know how I had deserved to be spared. I was ashamed, because I felt like a participant in this Injustice which was maiming children in Sarajevo the way bugs are killed underfoot.

Dad came in. Alma died. In Latin, Alma means soul. I want to write, as best as I can and as honestly as I know how, and I want to make this notebook into a colorful birdhouse for all the little souls which fly over us terrified by the fluttering of their own wings.

■ □ ■ □ ■

CHAPTER ONE

How we became lodgers. The Zone of the Fourth Dimension. First indications of a plot: a pocket mortar, Granny's little suitcase, a bet.

UNTIL APRIL OF THIS ONE THOUSAND NINE HUNDRED AND NINETY-second year, Sarajevo was known in the world for three things: the Winter Olympics; the assassination of the Archduke; and kebabs, coffee-shops, new-primitivism, football, Makarska, burek, and the folk who live here. Since April it has been known for just one thing. War. Although no one agrees when it began (I remember a conversation in Davor's Yugo. Davor said that the army was at the border, Sanja asked which army, and I which border?), the official date is the fourth of April. That day we were in our flat in the Dobrinje district. Mother, Granny, and I were alone. Dad had spent the night in the museum, believing the popular saying that the captain should be the last to leave his sinking ship. However, since the museum was not burnt down, and our flat was, in panic and at the last minute we moved in with Dad and became lodgers.

Then the telephones stopped working, and I lost contact with my friends. Our district was cut off; no one could go in or out. It was also divided. One part was occupied by Serbs. My literature teacher stayed in that part. The last time I spoke to him, when I told him I didn't know what to do, he had said: Write.

So, I'm writing.

In the museum we found my brother, Davor, and his expectant wife, Sanja. Their story is simple. In April planes had taken away people frightened by the war, which had already nestled down around Sarajevo. They were military planes without seats; people traveled in them sitting on the floor. Most of the planes went to Belgrade. Then the airport was closed. Then my brother stopped trying to persuade the expectant one that they should transplant themselves to another part of the planet. She didn't want to leave her doctors. Later she would discover that her doctors had left her. One was wounded, one flew away, and the third stayed on the Serbian side. The young married couple came to the museum, because their landlord had moved into their little basement room. Basements had suddenly become the most sought-after living space, because of the shells that were then being scattered over the town like confetti.

They brought with them their first child, their dog, Sniffy, a two-year-old aristocrat of the Dalmatian race. I say aristocrat because Mother had once observed that more was known about his ancestors and predecessors further back than about all of us in the museum put together.

Apart from our family, about whom I shall be writing some more in the following pages, two other people registered in the lodgers' club: Brkić, the porter, and his friend, Julio. Both of them had been Partizans in the previous war.

My name is Maja. What I am writing will be a novel in the form of a diary, or perhaps a new form—a diary in the form of a novel. I haven't decided yet. I'm writing it because there's nothing else for me to do. We don't go to school, we don't watch television, we don't leave the cellar. We don't leave the cellar because the war is up above us. The war is being waged between Serbs, Croats, and Muslims. Davor says that the war is being waged because the Croats have Croatia, the Serbs have Serbia, but the Muslims don't have Muslimia. Everyone thinks it would be right for them to have it, but no one can agree where the borders should be. Dad says that Davor is a dunce and that the war is being waged because the Serbs and Croats want to divide Bosnia and kill and drive out the Muslims. I don't know what to say. There are some things I don't get. For instance, why do the Serbs call armed Muslims who wear red fezzes *green berets*? Or, why do the Muslims call Serbs who wear red berets *white eagles*? What's the difference between Ustashas and Chetniks? (Chetniks have beards, which they wear like bibs. They look exactly like Orthodox priests, except that priests have bigger bellies. And Ustashas look like chimney sweeps.)

No! I don't think I'll be able to explain objectively and impartially to an average foreign reader why war is being waged here. Probably, like all wars, it's about taking territory and plunder. But I can't think of a *probably* for why a city of half a million inhabitants should be bombarded day after day from the surrounding hills. Why would anyone (in our case the Serbian artillery) destroy houses, burn libraries, and shatter minarets and the poplars planted around them?

Why, this spring, instead of cherries, are children collecting shrapnel and swapping it like marbles, picture-cards, or badges? Why, since we are, after all, already living in the museum, are we sleeping on civil defense stretchers, in the cold, damp cellar instead of on the beds of beys and wealthy Sarajevans? (I know the answer to the last question: because Dad has used our mattresses and quilts to stuff into the windows, with the aim of protecting the lodgers in case of sudden shelling.)

My dad is fifty years old and has one of the broadest partings in the city. (Stylistic figure: euphemism.) He is a historian by profession and the director of the museum. He has broad and slightly stooped shoulders. He has lost weight, and his clothes flop and hang around him. This makes him look untidy, although he is one of the rare men in this war, and the only one in the museum, who shaves regularly. (Maybe he has time to spare, because he rarely combs his hair?) In the first days of the war, he traveled through the whole town, to our house, and to the museum, hunting for fire-engines and dust-carts, to carry him, together with bunches of other crazy pedestrians, through the crossfire and smoking shell-falls. Thanks to that, I imagined the beginning of the war as a First of May parade of monuments that had come to life, in which bronze and marble Partizans with their legs and arms spread wide strove not to fall off their pedestals.

Another interesting personality is my mother. She is a vegetarian of the macrobiotic variety, although she sometimes sins by smoking over a coffee. She is slim thanks to yoga. (Yoga is the custom of saluting the sun before it appears by scratching one's ears with one's toes.) She gets up first and goes to bed last. (In fact, I only presume that she does actually sleep.) Over these last few weeks? months? years? she has made the museum begin to behave like a home.

The third interesting person is my brother, who is my mother's son, but not my father's. That is to say, my mother married more than once and less than three times. My brother, Davor, works for the Radio, as a director of radio plays, despite his degree in film direction. Radio plays are what you can hear on the radio when the television isn't working and when the first program is broadcasting classical and the second serious music. Of everything he has directed, I liked best a show called *Phantom,* when he himself appeared on the program and talked nonsense. For instance when he launched a campaign for the introduction of newly composed folk songs into school readers. I've even remembered one: *One day when I was sad, I met a handsome lad, He offered me a ring, And lovely white clothing, I was clothed by Raif, In silk and kadaif.*

I quoted this in order to mention one of his character traits, namely irony. He is always negatively inclined, finding something ugly, stupid, or primitive in everything. That's why he's sometimes tedious. He's tall, thin, wears glasses, and when he's not working at the Radio, his job is to serve his wife and annoy my father.

Since I've already mentioned my sister-in-law: she's in the fourth month of her pregnancy. That happened like this: As a graduate architect, she got a job at a garage, where one lovely sunny day she lifted up the windscreen wipers, wiped off the dead flies, and saw the face of her future husband, who was at that moment handing her his spectacles to clean as well. Afterward she admitted that she had fallen for his cow-like eyes. (I would have said ox-like.) That was also the last time that she washed and polished any glass in his presence.

Mother's mother, Greta, looks much older than she is, but she behaves as though she were much younger. This is mostly seen in the way she behaves at table, when she serves herself first, slurps, fights over the crust although she hasn't got any teeth, and always chooses the best bits although, in fact, she can hardly see. This gives her the right to stand at the table and poke her nose into every dish placed on it. She will not be parted from an old suitcase, which is in fact not a suitcase, but something between a chest, a tin cash-box, and a postmodern woman's vanity-case.

So, Granny can hardly see, but she hears virtually nothing. That's why she talks in a way that only practiced listeners can understand. The sentence "Today I went to buy a newspaper," in her interpretation would look like this: "Went paper, went buy buy paper today." (For my audience I shall give a simultaneous translation of her remarks.) It is strange how, nevertheless, when she thrusts her face right into yours, she understands everything you say to her perfectly.

My Granny is not the oldest of the lodgers in the museum. Brkić and Julio are older. Both of them are bony, gray-haired, and tall. Brkić wears a sweater and windbreaker, Julio a suit and coats. Brkic neglects his beard and mustache, Julio tends his. Brkić says little, Julio lots. Brkić has been in the museum since before the war, he worked here as a night porter. Julio came after a shell pierced his refrigerator, three rooms, and his doctoral thesis. The thesis was entitled *The Skoj Movement and Postwar Youth*.

I still haven't decided whether this is going to be a novel or a diary. In case it's a novel, I ought to start describing some events. Our literature teacher told us several times that you can't have a plot without events, and without a plot you can't have a story. Today two things happened that could be the beginning of a plot. (A plot is a series of events connected by causal-consequential relations and presented in chronological order.)

The first event occurred last night. Davor brought a tape recorder home. We all assembled in the porter's lodge, which was the most secure ground-floor space in the museum, because then we were separated from the shells by at least two thick walls and at least two concrete blocks. Davor had been given the task of making a radio program about us in the museum. Brkić immediately refused. He said that he didn't like microphones, even if he could see them while he was talking. Davor's wife said nothing, but you could see from her face that she resented the fact that her husband had chosen the radio, which was not in a position to convey all the difficulties she was having to put up with on her journey through her pregnancy. Granny said that other pregnant women were having a hard time as well. My sister-in-law replied that the fact that other pregnant women were having a hard time didn't make things any easier for her.

I also refused to participate in this tape-recording project. I made it quite clear to him that he could no longer count on me as a symbol of youthful views of the world, because, ever since the war had cut deep scars into my soul, I no longer considered myself, or felt, young. Besides, every day some pensioner or poet published an appeal in the name of hundreds and thousands of children, so why not ask them for assistance. In order that her son should not be left without a program at all, Mother offered to point out the detrimental effect of meat in the nutrition of human beings, the length of whose large intestine made them herbivores, but Davor begged her with a glance to stop before she had even begun.

That left Dad and Julio.

Dad is one of those people who even before going into the lavatory considers all the circumstances which determine whether this rather than that newspaper deserves to go with him. He would first sketch out what he wanted to say. Write a plan.

Davor would like to hear something about the first days of the war. When Dad opposed the local armed groups who burst into the museum to take exhibits of weapons as trophies.

They took only a Partizan machine-gun and a pocket mortar. All in all it wasn't worth talking about.

And so I got the opportunity to hear Julio. (Davor turned the tape recorder off after two minutes, because Julio talks like this: Us two was subtenants, and we pays two dinars, no, one dinar eighty, in rent, in advance, on the first of each month, and in those days our pay was seven and six that is thirteen, and five that is eighteen dinars and thirty paras, I knows because I remembers the list, like I can see it now, half in blue ink and half in red, there weren't any ballpoint pens then, people wrote with feathers, but there wasn't any ink, so people had to use their wits, I once squeezed the ink pads used for official stamps, and at that time we had stamps coming out of our ears. There wasn't a single desk without a stamp. Stamps for letters, stamps for contracts, stamps for certificates, stamps for entrance tickets, stamps for messages. If you're writing a love letter and don't have a stamp to seal it with, it's no good. What do you expect, a bunch of illiterates, so they likes to see official stamps. Where was I? Oh, yes, the two of us are subtenants. In Belgrade. After the war all the Partizans comes to Belgrade, that's routine, like a snooze after lunch. Anyone who didn't come to Belgrade after the war had problems later proving that he ever was in the war at all. And so, the two of us subtenants, in the center, the street's called, it's called . . . what's it called . . . Number seven, and it's named after some writer . . .)

Needless to say, for my readers I shall extract the essence. Julio and Brkić have known each other since the war. They were both Partizans. In Belgrade they fell in love with the same girl. She was suspected of having collaborated with the aggressor. (Germans at that time, so-called Krauts.) That meant she had given herself to them. Together they helped her get a passport and leave the country, and that got Brkić put in jail. Julio continued his career, and was a successful civil servant and diplomat, and when Brkić was released, he looked after him. He found him a job at a printer's, maintaining the machines. Then Julio became ambassador and Brkić made a barge and lived on it. Then Julio came back and settled in Sarajevo. Brkić's barge and everything on it were burned in a fire. Then Julio invited Brkić to join him and found him a job as porter at the museum. That was ten years ago. Now, at the end of their lives as at the beginning, both of them are proletarians.

. . . The street was named after Sima Matavulj, the Sarajevan.

Davor asked (you could see he was my brother) did they know what had happened to the girl, but then my sister-in-law came in and asked whether they were going to take much longer.

Why?

Because he had promised that morning that he would beat Sniffy's molting hairs out of the blankets and rugs, and clean his shoes. She would do it, but she couldn't, since she was protecting her pregnancy and had to rest. (In other words she shouldn't keep clambering up from the cellar every few minutes to ask him to come down.)

At times I am deeply touched and disappointed by the realization that my brother is shedding his talent in the form of hairs from blankets. And I am driven to despair by the thought of how many artists, as they made their way through the world, had been obliged to exchange their paintbrushes for shoe-cleaning supplies.

My brother then got up, turned off the tape recorder that had been off for an hour already, and went down to his married quarters.

His wife had not wanted, while it was still possible, to leave the town by plane or car. People considered her decision heroic. (Pregnant women are not usually considered idiots.) But the main burden, in my opinion, was borne by my brother. He listens to the news and tells her only the bearably terrible bits. He peels apples and eats the skin, cutting slices for her. He telephones to find medicines, diagnoses, and advice for her symptoms. He went to a friend to borrow weighing scales while there wasn't so much as a mattress in the museum. He was the first person in Sarajevo to begin to exchange American dollars for toilet paper. And finally, he was the only one to sit in the cellar when everyone else went out onto the streets in defiance, and the only one to go out into the streets, to find tablets, when everyone else was sitting in cellars out of fear.

My sister-in-law, Sanja, managed to convince us that their marriage was their problem, so that we watched our Davor from the other side of the table as though he were on the other side of a film screen. That's why I sometimes think he's right when he starts defending his theory that all of us here are hostages, equally, of those who are attacking us and of those who are defending us.

After the interview came to an end with Davor's departure, the third shift of gunners from the hills announced an attack, and one of the fiercest bombardments of the city began. We all dashed down to the cellar. Only Dad and Brkić stayed in the porter's lodge to watch out for fires. In the morning we found a hole in the wall above the main entrance, and on the floor under our feet, pieces of brick poking out of the carpet through the dust. If this turns out to be a novel, maybe I'll call it *Sky in the Wall*.

This war has been going on for nearly two months, and I still haven't described what it's actually like. That's because it's impossible to write while you're sitting in the dark, in the cellar, while the walls and foundations around you are shaking. And when, sometimes, it stops, then everything seems pointless. Especially keeping notes like this. However, today I have given myself my word.

There are large numbers of contradictory theories about who started this war and why it's happening, who is guilty and who innocent, who is defending, and who attacking. What is certain is that three nations are at war: Serbs, Croats, and Muslims. A foreign reader might well ask who they are and how they differ. Just as I might, for instance, wonder what the difference is between Boers and Pygmies.

I have thought for a long time about what the difference is between Serbs, Muslims, and Croats. They speak the same language, they lived in the same state, they had the same currency, they married each other. The only thing I could identify was faith. The Serbs are Orthodox, which means the others are Unorthodox. The Muslims are True Believers, which means the others are False Believers. The Croats are Catholics, which means that the others are Protestants. But if I try to go on being logical, that means that the war is being waged because of different faiths. That is, it is being waged by believers. Against whom? Against unbelievers. I've got muddled. I'd better write about what I can see.

And of everything that I see, in the half-dark behind the barred windows, between two mad dashes to the cellar, what I like best is what I used to come to the museum to see even before the war: the model of the old part of the town, the so-called *čaršija*. There everything is as it once was, and as it always was: narrow streets under broad eaves, tall minarets among poplars, and the tops of the lime trees round the Sahat-kula Clock Tower. I stand in front of the glass case and one moment I am myself somewhere down there, beside the shops, on the white cobblestones, in some other, nicer time, and the next I am again hovering over it all like an angel with tarred wings. I would call this phenomenon *The Fourth Dimension*.

The museum is not in the model for two reasons. First, because it was built later, under Austria, and secondly because it's on a rise outside the *čaršija* itself and above the part of it shown in the model.

The museum has two inner courtyards, or atria. The first, larger one, is lined by a colonnade, and behind the columns, in glass cases, are exhibits from the prehistoric period. In the middle of the atrium is a garden, with a *stećak* tombstone peering out of a rose bush. You get to the second courtyard, also rectangular, through the hall with the model in it and several other corridors and staircases. It's smaller, paved, and as though made in order to be transformed into a pleasant terrace for sitting about on. (Which the lodgers do.) The whole courtyard reminds one of the theaters where the audience used to watch the first nights of Shakespeare's plays. The poorer audience was able to enter the ground floor through several doors in the three outside walls, while the richer people watched through windows on the first floor, side by side round the whole courtyard.

The building was built in 1887, in the pseudo-Moorish style, designed by Karl Parzhik, as a Sheria law school. It has three entrances. The main one leads down steps to the old town. It's closed now. The side door leads into the garden belonging to the museum, while the trades entrance, beside the porter's lodge, leads into the street which is, theoretically, least exposed to the gun barrels on the hills. This is the one used by us, and the other people who come to our cellar.

In the cellar we sit on crates, wrapped in blankets. It all reminds one of traveling second class by night train. When a shell falls, the walls and floors rumble and glass shatters somewhere above us. We all huddle up, thrust our heads into our shoulders and our chins into the blanket, between our arms crossed on our chests. Even Granny, who keeps asking every quarter of an hour whether we're going upstairs, because she's bored. At least that's how it was before we got the television. Since she doesn't see well, she goes right up to the screen and it looks as though she's sniffing the picture, which would probably before the war have been described as interference on the wires or the wind has bent our antenna again.

That's why in the end Brkić fixed up an aerial of aluminum and copper wires, and Julio brought Granny binoculars, through which she can follow the program from what had been until yesterday an unimaginable distance of several meters. Now those who don't believe their own eyes can believe the television.

We made a bed for the expectant mother, on which she usually lies rigid, with an expression on her face indicating roughly that labor is about to begin. My brother sits beside her holding her hand. Sniffy keeps trying to wriggle in between them, under the blanket, of course. When they get cross with him and shoo him away, he walks off, taking the blanket that had been covering them with him. The credits of the film *Sniffy of Arabia* are shown several times in the course of the night.

Mother on the whole stands by the door waiting for Dad to come down. Julio sits and surveys Granny's game of patience. At the same time he talks to Brkić, who comes down from time to time to snatch a cigarette. Quite by chance I heard a conversation that could be the beginning of the plot, if I decide that what I'm writing will be a novel.

Money opens even iron doors. With his connections and acquaintances, Julio would be able to stop the war. If only he could get out of the city. Here, in the museum, there was jewelry, and antique coins, and postage stamps, and paintings, and old arms, everything . . . (Julio offered Brkić a half pack of cigarettes.) He wasn't thinking of plundering the museum, God forbid, he would just take a little. This was war, no one would notice. Put it down to a shell . . .

Not a chance. Not so long as Brkić was the caretaker.

Good for Brkić. What belonged to society, belonged to society. But there was private jewelry in the museum as well. For instance, Greta's little case. What did he think, how much could there be in it?

Really, what about my Granny's suitcase?

I asked Mother what Granny kept in it. She replied that she didn't know. The case was made of tin, black, smaller than a briefcase, with a lock that Granny kept padlocked. She kept the key on a chain round her neck. From the blazing flat she had taken only a bag and this tin vanity case. I know that she left albums of photographs, bundles of letters, and documents behind. She wore her jewelry and carried little bottles of perfume in her bag. I don't know what else could be hidden inside the black tin.

Julio tried to talk me into it. If it were true that Jews were rich, and my granny was Jewish, then it wasn't entirely out of the question that my family had some treasure, which I was not supposed to know about until I was twenty-one. That would explain why my mother refused any discussion of this matter.

Brkić didn't peer into other people's suitcases.

If you took everything into account, Greta owed them.

I didn't understand this bit. Perhaps I hadn't heard right. They had begun to talk more softly. Then Brkić put out his half-smoked cigarette, which is a fairly rare occurrence. (Like me leaving half a piece of chocolate!) Before he went, Julio offered him his hand: Wanta bet?

Brkić accepted, and went out.

CHAPTER TWO

Aladdin's cave. How to make meat from flour. Fifth-column hunters?
The Icon-savior. *Umbra!* Mistress of memories.

ALTHOUGH EVERYONE THOUGHT AND SAID THAT THE WAR WOULD BE over soon, it's still going on. What we had been afraid of is happening. We are getting used to explosions, whistling shells, pandemonium, and humiliation. To life in the cellar.

Today Dad wrote his plan for his presentation on Davor's program. We heard his typewriter. Dad had found the machine, a noble *Adlerverke von Frankfurt,* and bought it for the museum, but he kept it, repaired and cleaned, for the Director's office. It took up as much room on the surface of his desk as an ordinary little typewriter, but it was three times taller and five times heavier. Its roller was far wider, which I put down to the length of German words. Mrs. Adlerverke was all in black, apart from what was nicest about her: the little round white keys with little glass circles stuck over the signs. The letters it made on the paper were nice, too. If what I'm writing here is ever printed, I would like it to be done in letters like those.

As I watched him sitting at his big desk, the wood of which could be used nowadays to furnish a whole nursery school, it occurred to me that we had been living in the museum for more than a month already.

If my literature teacher were here, he would have enough subjects for the next twenty school essays: Who had sat at that desk where Dad was now writing? What were all the documents that had been signed at that desk? What had the craftsman made apart from that desk?

Dad was sitting there. The window was barricaded with precious oriental rugs, just a few cracks let in rays of light. The advantage of blockaded windows is that at every time of day they give an impression of dawn. In one room, where Brkić had set up his residence, we had put away all the exhibits of old weapons. For me the most interesting things were the long rifles with which you could keep your enemy at a distance even without ammunition. In another room were pictures. In a third, embroidery and textiles, traditional costumes, scarves, silk. Next to them were crystal, dishes, gilt and silver goblets, jugs, candlesticks, a menorah, cutlery in leather boxes with monograms on their lids.

This is how one might imagine Aladdin's cave.

Several rooms had been left for the collections of furniture; one had been turned into a library; in one there were herbals, albums, donations from philatelists, collectors of insects and butterflies, old letters, postcards, and coins. Then photograph albums, retired cameras, plans and sketches of buildings, objects from old craft shops.

I have listed all this although in lessons I had not been a supporter of Balzac's literary procedure. I did it in order that the reader should understand what Dad wrote and later read into Davor's microphone.

He compared the Serbs to the Vandals, the tribe which destroyed Rome. I've forgotten the year. The shelling of the museum could have been ordered only by someone who was just as primitive as the person who carried out the order. The Serbs on the hills were war criminals. They were capable of destroying in one night what had been preserved for us over the centuries through many wars. The devastation which our city and the Independent Republic of Bosnia and Herzegovina had suffered was already greater than in the whole four years of the last world war.

Davor turned off the tape recorder.

Dad stopped reading and looked at him enquiringly.

Davor didn't want to make a propaganda program.

Ecce homo! Why was it propaganda?

Because it wasn't objective. And since when had our republic been independent?

Since the day when the world recognized it as such and when it proclaimed itself as such.

What had it been doing since that day? Just running around begging for charity. It depended on foreign aid, on foreign intervention, on foreign support. That same America was behaving like a drunken registrar! It had married the young couple, although only one party agreed to the marriage. And the reason why the city was being destroyed was because there was an army in that city. Before they had set up their mortar in front of our museum, not a single shell had fallen on it. If Dad and Brkić had not been here from the first day, the people on the hills wouldn't have had a chance to destroy or burn anything. Thieves from the city would have taken it all and distributed it among themselves.

When Davor had finished, Dad, who had not for one moment altered his enquiring look, glanced at me. (His glance meant: Have I heard right? If I have, then which of the two of us is sane?) I turned my page and went on pretending to read. After a quarter of an hour I got up and went out, letting them know that they had got back to the chicken and the egg for the nth time. People kept talking about why the war started and whose fault it was. I still hadn't heard anyone say how the war could be stopped and who would do it.

When I went into the atrium, I found Brkić cleaning a pistol. Two cigarettes were burning in an ashtray, a third in his mouth. I wanted to ask him a bit about Granny, just to clarify what it was that she might owe him and Julio, when two defenders of the city entered, followed by Julio, with his brand new accreditation, and in front of them all a tall man with a mustache, who was their commander.

Here it will be necessary to explain what accreditation is. Accreditation is a piece of paper in a plastic cover which hangs from the lapel. The difference between a person with one of these attached to him and a person without it is the difference between a family pet and a stray dog. Although looking at the accreditation has replaced looking into the eyes, I still noticed that one of the newcomers was cross-eyed. This turned out to be awkward, because there was no way I could be sure which of his two eyes was looking at me, and which one of my two he was addressing. As nature had endowed him also with a large, sticking out chin, he asked questions over it, as over rifle sights.

Neither of them was in uniform, but they both had new gym shoes and guns. The younger and shorter one, with sunglasses, in a black jacket, and with a coat of arms on a band round his head, sat down at once. The other one, whom I called Clarence, after the lion in the TV series, couldn't decide which of the one remaining chair to choose. The barrel of his automatic was not pointed at the floor or the sky, but at us. This made me a little nervous. Then Mother arrived.

The commander asked whether we were aware that the fifth column was operating in the city.

In what way? asked Mother, in the tone of a psychiatrist trying to help an acute lunatic.

To the surprise of all present, it was Julio who answered: In every way. Snipers, window blinds, flashlights, radio stations, clothes, telephones, signals . . .

How many of us were there in the museum? Clarence asked. Both Mother and I had just opened our mouths to answer the question, when it was answered by Dad, who had just come in and was the person to whom the question was addressed. He listed us all. Then he showed his identity papers. Clarence didn't even look at them. He went out of the door through which Dad had just come in. Sanja followed him out. I heard her informing him that he would be able to enter her room only if he took off his Jugosport gym shoes first.

The tall policeman then explained why they had come. His colleague, he said, pointing at Julio, had offered rooms for the use of the headquarters of the Territorial Defense, TD for short. They had come to have a look. Dad sent a meaningful glance in the direction of the colleague, but Julio decided just then to wipe the dust from his new accreditation.

Did the gentleman know that this was a museum?

And did the Director know that this was a war? What was the use of a museum if there were no longer a city?

What was the use of the city if it didn't have a museum?

And is a state of use? Independent, sovereign, indivisible, free, secular . . .

Let the gentleman take the headquarters to his own house.

It's been destroyed.

Then let him put up a tent in a park. And there were still free hills round the city. And he, Dad, would report this conversation the next day to the Ministry of Culture and the City Hall.

Then Clarence came back, with the information that the upper floor had an excellent view. I immediately imagined him holding a special pair of binoculars in his hand, with eye-pieces at a right angle. He also said to be careful of light. If he saw a bulb lit anywhere, he would shoot at the window. Without warning. For our own good.

When they left, Dad asked their colleague, Julio, what was going on. Why had *umbra* come to the museum. (I thought that UMBRA was a secret Macedonian information service. But it wasn't. *Umbra* was one of Dad's favorite Italian expressions. It means shadow, but it also designates an uninvited guest.) Their colleague sat down, took a tray with coffee from Mother's hands, handed out the cups, and offered us cigarettes. It turned out, between slurps, that he had brought them.

That's what they said themselves.

He had brought them so that they could see for themselves that the museum wasn't suitable for their headquarters.

In response to that lie, Dad said *non olet* (it doesn't smell right), inhaled deeply, and went out to exhale somewhere else. Granny, the worker bee, sucked the rest of the nectar from his cup.

I was curious and asked how the fifth column summoned the enemy artillery with clothes and window blinds.

Simple. There's a book about it, based on actual events in London. It's by, it's by . . . I can just see the book. Thin, blue cover, no, red. Or half-blue, half-red. No, those were the pencils, the pencils were half-blue, half-red, like the pencils he used for underlining when he was in school. Blue for what was right, and red for what was wrong. No . . .

In short. Clothes are used to signal like this: if you wear black, it means the target wasn't hit. White means it was. Black on top and white underneath, they had undershot. White on top and black underneath, they had overshot. And blinds, if they're pulled halfway down, mean don't attack here. Then, burning rubbish, smoke signals, flushing water in the lavatory according to the Morse code, and then someone in the neighborhood would pass the signal on.

Who knows how much longer I would have borne the consequences of my careless curiosity, had not Brkić interrupted him and
told him not to talk rot. And then he asked him what that was
hanging over his heart.

Accreditation.

Why?

So people would know he's guarding the museum.

So where's one for him?

There isn't one. There was only one. There has to be a file. Since
everyone who has accreditation gets free coffee, sugar, oil . . .

So what did he get?

Coffee.

How much?

Half a kilo.

Where is it, we'll grind it. (This was Granny's suggestion. Once
again my suspicions that she is a medical phenomenon have been
confirmed. She can't see or hear, but she knows exactly what's going
on as soon as food or drink is mentioned.)

It's gone. I gave it away.

Who to?

To the man who fixed my accreditation.

Brkić glanced at him, inhaled, and went to exhale somewhere
else. Mother was pleased. The illusion of this deceptive material
world of ours had been confirmed once again. Granny was not
pleased. Her binoculars had disappeared.

The careful reader will note that I mentioned two Territorial
Defenders, but described only one. This is because the other one
deserves a little more attention and space. The first thing I noticed
about him was his enormous conceit. I don't know whether he
owed this to his courage, his resemblance to Tom Cruise, or something else. This would not have concerned me, had I not caught
him several times staring at me. (Probably he couldn't believe that
anyone's ears, even droopy ones like mine, could bear the burden of
such thick spectacle lenses.) So that no one should think that I have
spent the afternoon endeavoring to explain to the poor paper why I
considered it necessary to devote more space than he deserves to an
extra, I shall describe the kitchen in which I am now sitting and
writing.

Before the war this was the place from where coffee was carried to the rooms and offices and sometimes receptions. Now, thanks mostly to Mother's devotion, it has been reorganized as the living room, in which, when the nights are quiet, she, Dad, and I sleep. There are two large beds and one small one, a wash-basin, a large walnut cupboard, a six-sided table made of rosewood, and an electric cooker. That's all the furniture. This little space is now also the place where food is baked, fried, dried, and boiled for eight people, of whom Granny eats and the expectant one helps herself for two.

As I have already warned the careful reader, Mother is a leader in the field of macrobiotic nourishment. One of the dishes we make is called *sejtan*. It's made with wholemeal flour, mixed with water, which is then drained. In this process of rinsing, the starch is separated from the albumen. When it's ready, the albumen, the *sejtan*, looks like a well-used kitchen sponge. That's what it tastes like, too. It's cut into sections, rolled in breadcrumbs, seasoned, and fried. Everyone who eats it, to please Mother, confirms that it's just like eating cutlets.

While we were rinsing the dough, I asked Mother what Granny kept in her suitcase. She replied with a counter-question, why did I want to know. Apart from the fact that every normal writer must want to know what someone keeps in a locked tin trunk, sleeping on it like a pillow, and putting her slippered feet on it while she tans her face on the cathode tube, I couldn't think of a better reason.

Which was why I was punished with a pedagogical essay:

People have a right to their secrets, and it's everyone else's duty to respect that right. If she felt it were necessary, Granny would open the case in front of me. If I were really interested, I could ask Granny. All in the conditional. All that was left for me was to turn up my nose and on that account not eat the battered sponges.

Then between half-past four and twenty-five to five, they started shelling the center of town again, as a result of which we all went down to the cellar. There we found my sister-in-law crying. Mother and her husband didn't try to comfort her, and Granny glued her nose to the screen, because of the static.

When Sanja cries, it's like rain in the autumn: the more you plan to go out, the harder it rains. My sister-in-law cries the way Mother does yoga, or the way I write, or Granny watches television. I cry, therefore I am. (Lat.: *ploro, ergo sum.*) Yesterday she cried because she had discovered that she did not have enough amniotic fluid for the baby. (She had probably cried half of it away.) The day before she cried because she had gained two kilograms more than the tables predicted. The day before that she cried because she had been constipated for five days. The day before that she cried because she had eaten a whole packet of cookies and a whole bar of chocolate. (Although it should have been me crying because I didn't get anything at all!) Some day I'll write an essay about crying. It'll be called "The Big Weep." Now she was crying, as I succeeded in discovering, because it was time for her to go for her ultrasound checkup, but it was impossible to go. Davor's Yugo had been pinched by good thieves so that it wouldn't be punctured by shells, while Dad's Beetle had been pinched by Dad himself so that it wouldn't be pinched by thieves or snipers. And even if they did make it up there, to the hospital, it wasn't certain that the ultrasound machine would be working.

None of that was her problem.

Of course, whatever was not her problem, became my brother's. She calmed down a bit after she was promised that they would certainly go that week for the checkup. I grabbed a moment in the course of the evening to inform my brother of my dissatisfaction and concern over his status in this marriage.

What status?

I listed: the status of foot masseur, dishcloth, razor, paper handkerchief, foot towel, mechanical answering machine, extension lead, coffeepot handle, wool-winding prop, mirror, mirror on the wall . . .

He interrupted me when I got to coffeepot handle: That checkup should have been done long ago, and Sanja had every right to be worried.

I asked him how, and when, and by what means he thought of going.

He didn't answer.

An opportunity to mention: Everything that was my brother's problem, was also my mother's problem. I have heard and read of the love which mothers feel and nurture toward their first-born or only sons, but this, in whose shadow I am growing up, deserves scientific observation.

My mother can't go to sleep until Davor gets back from town. For Davor dinner is produced even at midnight. It cannot happen that he feels like having a shower, and there is no hot water. Everything he mislays, Mother finds. He is not obliged to do his own washing-up. For her he is always tired and ought to lie down and rest a little. He has fought for the right for no one to enter his room, so that his writing or thinking aren't interrupted. Not even his marriage, when he moved out of our house, nor the war, which left us without a home, diminished these uncontrollable and unjust responses on my mother's part. That is why I was surprised at her suggestion that she should go and bring the doctor to the museum??! (Two question marks and an exclamation are punctuation marks expressing astonishment.)

Dad observed that for an ultrasound check you needed an appropriate machine as well as a doctor.

Mother knew that. But if children were born a hundred years ago without ultrasound, this one could be as well. There are doctors who give a more accurate diagnosis with their fingers than with an ultrasound sensor. For instance, they told an acquaintance of hers, and her daughter, that she was going to have a boy and she produced two little girls. A waste of ten blue sleepers. They had to exchange the bottles for others, with pink tops.

Julio remembered that they had told one woman, after her ultrasound examination, that she was in the twenty-eighth rather than the thirtieth week of pregnancy. She got married in a rush, to the wrong man.

Mother looked gratefully at Julio and served him another cupful of pudding. That was why we didn't hear the continuation of his ultrasound reminiscences.

I must admit that at that moment I felt sorry for the lonely expectant one. In the last analysis, she was here, among us, like in a foreign camp. Without her mother, or her father, or her brother, she didn't go out anywhere, no one came to see her, of course she was afraid. I would be nice to her the next day.

Davor didn't wait until the next day. He snuggled his wife up in a blanket and stroked her hair, until she soon calmed down and fell asleep.

Then the walls started to shake. The sound you hear as you sit in the cellar of the museum, onto which shells are falling, is like the one made by people in the flat above you moving a bookshelf or piano for hours from one corner of the room to another. Dad left after the first round. Julio and Brkić went with him. But Julio came back at once, picked up his first-aid kit and sat down by the door. From there he could intervene if anything happened to anyone up there or if one of us down here was taken ill.

And Davor stayed beside Sanja. He didn't even try to get up.

Davor is neither lazy nor a coward. Few would bet that out of twelve throws of a dice not once would there be a six. But he, from the beginning of the war until today, going to work and coming home, through triumphal arches of gun fire, has agreed to such an arrangement with destiny. He told Dad simply that he was not going to save things only for others to take them and sell them.

That's why Dad didn't count on him anymore. And that evening, through all the crashing and flashing, he decided to put the icons away! (Icons are pieces of wood covered in paint that has dried and cracked. They have pictures on them of Serbian volunteers holding in one hand a cross, or a staff, or a book, or a key, or something similar, and with the other shaking a threatening finger at someone.) Mother was proud because of that. Her husband, a Muslim, was saving Serbian icons from the Serbs who wanted to destroy them in order to save them from the Muslims. (Whenever both Serbs and Muslims find themselves together in one sentence, that sentence is illogical. For how can anything be saved by being destroyed?)

Davor explained to me that the Serbs came down from the surrounding hills to help their own people in the town. Do they help them by howitzering and tanking them, like everyone and everything else? (Did the reader notice that "came down from the hills"? From where? From heaven? Is that why they call themselves a *heavenly people*? Or, for example, Kosovo. That's a meadow in Serbia on which in a war with the Turks six hundred years ago, all the Serbs were killed. Only some Branko or other was saved. That's why all Serbs now call themselves Branković. I'm kidding.)

Although I don't particularly feel like writing, I must finish off yesterday, because I still haven't decided whether this is going to be a novel or a diary.

With Brkić's help, Dad laid the icons on his bed, on which he no longer slept in any case, in the cellar. Julio helped them with advice, because he wasn't able to abandon his little first-aid bag. One suggestion was that he and Dad should organize an auction: the icons would be bought up by the blue berets (soldiers of the United Nations, who are doing something or other in Sarajevo) like hot cakes. And they'd share the profits. Dad would get half for the museum and Julio half for the continuation of the armed struggle. Julio would organize it all.

Mother served the icon-saviors with the above-mentioned pudding. Brkić went to wash his hands, and when he came back, he found his bowl empty. Julio told him that he was wrong not to have tried it, because the pudding was divine. Granny was licking her lips. Dad offered Brkić his cup. Julio again showed himself the gentleman and Dad's pudding as well found itself in front of Granny. Granny smiled at Julio, and then moved from smiling to action. For the next ten seconds we all pretended not to hear the slurping, lapping, and swallowing.

I asked Mother why Granny ate like that.

How?

As though she were hungry and needy. I remember that she had on several occasions eaten chocolate which I had been hiding from myself, with great self-denial and psychological turmoil, during long days of unsuccessful diets. Her eyesight's bad and her hearing even worse, I don't believe that she uses her sense of taste, because she simply gulps down anything and everything. But on the other hand her sense of smell is developed to an extent that often borders on the incredible.

For instance, she knows, even before the door opens, which of the lodgers has returned to the museum. She gives a weather forecast with infallible accuracy, based on the intensity of the stench from the sewers. Mother and she, half joking, half seriously, were considering opening an agency for interpreting character and destiny on the basis of bodily aromas. Granny was on the whole responsible for what Mother prided herself on—our men's habit of changing their underwear daily, even in these circumstances. She was the first to voice the suspicion that in the market they were selling detergent mixed with flour. The pastry in the washing machine filter proved her right. It was from her that I heard that people sweat in one way when they are happy and satisfied, and in another when they are upset and anxious.

But what knocked me sideways were her stories about perfumes. Granny married once, my grandfather, but she lived with several men. (Never at the same time, don't get me wrong.) One of them, her first love, was the son of a German pharmacist. She spent several years with him.

She told me about fields of grass and hills of rose petals, of large rooms with glass balloons and pipes, about people whose job it was to create scents, about soaps and scented salts, about artists who sculpted shapes for bottles and boxes.

Once I found her, in my room, with several red currants squashed between her thumb and forefinger. In her lap she had my jacket. Or rather, not exactly mine, but my friend's, which I had borrowed, because it was smeared with machine oil in a refined way, which you couldn't buy anywhere and this made it very fashionable. Then she confessed that she was already losing her memory. Or, to be more precise and not lazy, something like this:

You don't forget reminiscences. They are always present. Like old letters in drawers. But the drawers are locked, and the keys get lost. Old people, who rarely go out, who move about in a confined space among familiar things, have no reason to revive a reminiscence which is waiting to be rediscovered in some drawer of the memory. (When I come to write an essay about memory and reminiscences, I must not forget to use the above sentence.)

But for her, for my Granny, it is enough to rub something between her fingers, or to scratch a stain with her nail, or to press her face into some material, and before her, like the spirit from Aladdin's lamp, arise images from the forgotten album of her long life. And here, too, in the museum, in the hours without light or electricity, I tend to find her sprinkling liquids from several different little bottles onto small lace handkerchiefs, swiftly and with an abrupt movement, so as not to spill more than necessary. And it occurred to me that she had, hidden from us, several bundles, not containing perfumes and extracts, but powders and shavings, which, when they were mixed with water or something similar, if I had understood properly, were able to revive the aroma of a cellar from her childhood, her father's trunk or the family attic, the wall of a house or a piece of rotten fence, overgrown with nettles. If that were the case, my Granny was not yet ready to give up her right to reminiscences. On the contrary, perhaps, when no one was watching her and we had all forgotten about her, she went around scratching things, making new stores of dust for her future journeys into the past.

Granny had left the empty bowl on her little case-table. Julio leapt up, and as though the little case were not a table but a tray, he picked them all up together. As though he were going to take it away. However, Granny got up as well: thank you, she'd do it herself.

That was one of the first attempts I witnessed to discover the contents of the little suitcase-treasure-trove.

■ □ ■ □ ■

CHAPTER THREE

Ultrasound and embroidered diapers. Dream of plum blossom. Barge on the Sava. Mahatma Hendrix. The trial of the Little Miljacka. Theft of Granny's suitcase. Phone call for Hamlet.

DAVOR SPENT THE WHOLE MORNING TRYING TO GET THROUGH TO someone at the hospital. The connections were bad. Some local telephone exchanges had been destroyed, we learned from unreliable sources. Between those that had stayed whole the cables had been destroyed. Hence it was mainly possible to telephone people you could also call to from your window.

In the end Davor established that the hospital was working and that ultrasound scans were being carried out. Then came the problem of transport. Whoever had a car, had no gas, whoever had gas, had no car. (Stolen, totaled, or burnt out.) And just as his enthusiasm was beginning to wane, Julio appeared: why hadn't he asked him first? He had a car. And what's more he had a friend working up there, in the hospital. Pete Bringforth.

He called the Territorial Defense headquarters: Did they know the city maternity hospital was running out of diapers? Well, it was. But there's all sorts of stuff in the museum, some embroidered, some not. When he was in the Partizans, that's how they got all they needed. So, it has to get to the maternity hospital. By car.

They'd be here in an hour.

Mother didn't want to eavesdrop, but if there was anything connected with her son, her ears turned in that direction of their own accord: It would be good if Julio were to wait for the Director to come back. After all, museum property should not be removed without his approval.

Julio remembered some lessons from Marxism, and started to demonstrate that a shirt decreased in value the older it was.

Mother knew that according to Marx all things decreased in value with time, it was only Marxists like him, Julio, who were supposed to appreciate. But she could not permit anything to be taken away until her husband had been asked. (Dad went every day, whether there was pounding—shelling—or a lull, to meetings of the directors of museums and galleries. There, instead of salaries, they got cigarettes, jeans, bags of jelly, and pepper and all sorts of other necessities without which one could do in wartime.)

Then Julio winked at her, telling her not to panic for nothing, because they would load the van with empty packing cases.

My mother is sometimes charming in her naive innocence. She glanced at Julio, and then asked what they would say at the hospital when they opened the cases and saw that they were empty.

Julio explained patiently that they weren't expecting any diapers at the hospital. He had made it up.

Mother understood as rapidly as she closed her mouth. That is, she didn't understand anything. My mother, a devotee of Vedic teachings, Yoga, Saibaba, Oshava, and so on, who salutes both the sun and our closest neighbors with equal devotion, doesn't cope too well in the colorful world of lies.

When Julio's comrades-in-arms, the so-called Territorials, arrived, the packing cases were ready. And Sanja and Davor were ready as well. And so was Dad, who had returned in the meantime and to whom Mother had recounted the whole thing the way she had digested it. Dad asked the gentlemen why they had come. Did the gentlemen have a warrant?

The gentlemen did not recognize the irony in the word *gentlemen,* and they replied. As they did so, the two gentlemen, of whom one had a narrow band over his forehead, and the other a still narrower forehead, had already picked up one packing case.

They didn't have a warrant, but they had weapons. And did the Director have a heart?

Why?

Because the Aggressor had left the babies without diapers. (The Territorials usually called their enemies, the Serbs, by the abbreviation Chetniks, but when they were speaking to educated people on an equal footing, they also called them Aggressors.)

That was no reason to leave the museum without exhibits, and the city and the country without its cultural heritage.

The Director shouldn't upset himself, as long as they were there, the Aggressor wouldn't come near the museum, let alone take anything from it.

There are various kinds of aggressors.

The Director shouldn't worry; they'd learned to recognize them.

Even in their own ranks?

Fifth column? Why, those were the sweetest!

So, what would they do if they saw someone taking packing cases out of the museum?

They'd check his papers. To see whether he was legitimate. And then they'd call him, the Director, to see what was being removed.

And what if someone saw them taking things out of this museum? Who?

Anyone. Neighbors, journalists, other Territorials.

The Director shouldn't be afraid, they all knew each other. And everyone would congratulate him for thinking about the babies.

Dad saw that he would have to change the way the conversation was going: He was sorry, and he was afraid that there had been some sort of misunderstanding, but he had neither the right nor the authority to dispose of the museum's holdings.

He wasn't disposing of anything, he was giving it to the maternity hospital.

OK, let's say that was it, but he still didn't have the right to give away something that didn't belong to him.

So who did it belong to?

The city.

The maternity hospital belongs to the city as well.

Dad mumbled *cantare surdo*, which in Latin means singing to the deaf, and then tried again: Were they quite OK? Were they in their right minds? Whoever heard of making diapers out of embroidered shirts, preserved for a hundred years?

And whoever heard of shooting a maternity hospital? But there was shooting. You couldn't get near it. There were no diapers, medicine, oxygen cylinders . . .

Nevertheless, Dad could not allow . . .

And he didn't have to! A moment ago he said they didn't belong to him.

He was responsible for them. He had given the weapons, he wasn't giving the shirts. *Placet!* (Resolved, Lat., I've decided. That's how all the European rulers ended their judgments.)

Mother got involved: She had given birth and put diapers on babies. The shirts were hard. They weren't suitable. Especially the embroidered ones . . .

OK, then let them take out the embroidered ones.

Julio leapt up: Let them take them all, there were experts up there, doctors, midwives, they'd be able to say what would work and what wouldn't.

But, too late. The packing case was already open. From it gaped its empty depths. The Territorials looked enquiringly at Julio, Julio at Mother: Had Madam thought they wouldn't check the cases?

Mother opened her mouth to defend herself, but then she probably realized she didn't know what from.

How could Madam do such a thing, when she herself was about to become a grandmother? How could she have allowed her husband to be exposed to all this unpleasantness? What was she thinking of? Keeping the clothes for her daughter? How disgraceful. So much for state possessions, when all the time . . .

Mother looked helplessly, first at Dad, then at Julio. Her eyes were full of tears. Julio gave Davor a signal. In a few moments he returned with a bundle of white shirts, which he threw into the packing case.

Dad asked Davor if he knew what he was doing.

Instead of an answer, Brkić appeared: Who was taking those shirts and where?

To be washed, muttered Julio.

I forgot, Brkić was holding a pistol in his hand.

The Territorial was not afraid. At least he didn't show it. He was probably surprised that, at his age, Brkić was in a position to hold himself up, let alone wield a pistol: Did the gentleman know that he needed a permit for a weapon?

Yes.

And did he have a permit?

No.

So why had he not handed his weapon into the nearest headquarters of the Territorial Defense?

Because he had never handed it over to anyone, and he wasn't going to start now.

They were obliged to take it from him.

Let's see them try.

The barrels of their guns were aimed at the ceiling, his at the floor. The Commander and Brkić looked each other in the eye for a time, until the former eventually turned his gaze on Julio. Who was already on the point of intervening. He would answer for Brkić. He was a bit edgy, he was old and ill, he was irascible, he didn't have any medicine . . .

While he was saying these things and others, he closed the packing case with the shirts in it, and sent the Territorials to carry it out. When I remember it all, it seems to me that Dad watched the whole process in silence, mostly because of Brkić. Because, had he continued to defend his shirts, Brkić would probably have stood in front of them, and the barrels would probably have been lowered. And raised. Fear of weapons sometimes does more harm and injustice than the weapons themselves.

As though in passing, Julio asked them to take Sanja and Davor as well. The girl had to have a check. I don't know what would have happened if they had refused. But they didn't. They were a bit confused themselves by then. Only the main one grunted something about an attack on the maternity hospital. Advance warning.

Mother put some powder called *vibhuti* on her finger and made a mark with it on Sanja's third eye. Davor moved out of the way, of course. Mother had to whisper one of her most potent mantras for him. A mantra is something like dialing a telephone number after which a telepathic connection is established with the Teacher, to whom one can then turn with a request as in a deposition. Mother once explained it to me: One shouldn't pray to Him to do something for us, for instance make us get a good mark for math, but to help us to do it ourselves.

That was why, in her kimono, white stockings, and Japanese slippers, with a knitting needle in her silver bun, she passed through this whole nightmare like a blossoming cherry tree through a downpour on the slopes of Mount Fuji. Her mantras were the wax in Odysseus's ears. She knew that in this life she had to serve and live for others, and she bore that burden on her shoulders like a brightly colored butterfly. Her faith transformed blots into adornments, faults into advantages, pain into joy. Everything that happened had a purpose and for some reason was good. Even this war was for her not the result of someone's stupidity, malice, and greed, but a measure of her and our spiritual and material poverty.

There was no meat, eggs, milk, cheese, butter. People ate bread soaked in oil and vegetable stock cubes, or they chewed doughnuts dunked in tea. Mother smiled, it was good, at last we were eating healthy food. She picked various grasses and roots round the museum, mixed up pastes from her golden reserves, and there—the flour we ate had the taste and appearance of normal food.

Mother thinks that food is just one of the ways in which our body acquires the energy it needs. The other two are love and the sun. What does our body do with this energy? It accumulates it, as potatoes do starch. What uses it and how? Our spirit, in its intergalactic journeys.

Food is, therefore, fuel. If the fuel is not good, the motor is ruined. And that leads to illness. The people say: Health comes in through the mouth. That's why Mother takes care that bad fuel, or extreme food, such as meat, alcohol, eggs, southern fruit, and everything else normal people eat, doesn't find its way to our table. But, one can read more about it all in the agitprop brochures of the Macrobiotic International.

Mother arrived at her calm through the practice of yoga and meditation. But, as before all other prophets and saints, God had placed before her a weighty trial, her son, Davor. In her dream of blossoming cherries, Davor behaved like a virus in a computer. That is, he didn't behave at all: he just stood, like a warped mirror.

Dad followed her out and went to his study to write a letter of protest. I stayed to hear Brkić explaining to Granny where and why the bridal pair had gone. When she realized that they had not gone to help Julio bring food, she went back to playing patience.

Patience is a game for one or more people. One person plays and the others get annoyed. Some get annoyed because the person is playing slowly, and others, like Dad for example, because anyone is playing at all. The only thing that excites Dad more than smoking is playing cards, and of all the card games there are it was patience that gave Julio the fiercest rash. Davor, Sanja, and I stand around Granny and cheer her on, while Dad grumbles: People are dying, and we're gawping at stupid girls and policemen. What's this game called?

Granny saw nothing of this. She sat, her little case on her knees, with miniature cards scattered over it. The game showed that everything would be all right with Davor and Sanja.

Brkić asked me what I was writing. I told him. He seemed to be favorably inclined toward my work, and that gave me a chance to ask him a few questions. I was interested in how someone like Julio could be his friend.

What's wrong with him?

I mentioned seventy-eight thousand failings.

You love your friends for their failings. (I thought this logic was strange, but the more I think about it, the more sensible it seems.)

I also asked about their shared love. That girl who was a lodger in the same house as the two of them.

How did I know about that?

Julio told me.

What did he tell me?

That she had been accused of collaboration. That they had helped her, and that after that he was arrested, and Julio transferred.

Did I know why he had been arrested? (Of course I didn't know.) Because Julio had denounced him. So as to intercede for her.

Why? Why had Julio done that?

So as to be left alone with the girl. But life is full of laughter.

Because he had denounced a comrade, he was promoted and had to leave Belgrade.

In his little porter's lodge-room, Brkić had a rucksack. It was made out of tarpaulin from a German truck. The rucksack had leather tapes and belts and three pockets also trimmed with leather. That rucksack contained his entire property. Among other things, a little cardboard box with several dozen fragile black and white photographs. Looking at them and asking him questions, I managed to piece together the story of his life:

In the Second World War, he'd been a member of the League of Young Communists, a Partizan, an officer. After the war, the romance with the girl and prison. He left prison after two years. He worked as a laborer, a builder, a lathe-operator. He took advantage of the first opportunity to retire. He had been married once, he even had a son somewhere. He had made one of the first houseboats on a raft in Belgrade. Well-known actors, singers, and writers used to come to that raft. Fish-soups simmered, well-chilled wine was drunk. One night the barge caught fire and burned right down to its metal fittings. All that Brkić was able to save was the rucksack, with its three pockets trimmed with worn leather. (I think my teacher would be pleased. I had succeeded in separating out of a life what was essential, in using verbatim descriptions, such as the well-chilled wine or the simmering. I was particularly pleased with the so-called framework composition—I had begun and ended with the rucksack, which could be seen as a symbol of his adventurous life.)

This was the first occasion on which I had heard him use complex sentences. As he talked about the barge and the Sava, his eyes shone. He repeated several times that you could never see enough of a human face and the starry sky.

The steel ring around the city and the museum must have been particularly hard for him, who had fought for freedom and paid for that freedom his whole life.

One day he'd get out of here, he'd find a way, he'd get some old comrades together, and drive that rabble away.

How did he think he could get out?

If he were younger, he'd break out. Ten artillery pieces were enough to hold back a company, but too little for one man. But now he'd have to think of something different.

I recalled something that Dad had once told me. I asked him whether he had worn a star on his forehead in the war?

Yes. A five-pointed red one . . .

Dad had read that starfish, five-pointed, ate by winding their stomachs round fish. The fish swam on, with the starfish slowly digesting them. Sometimes he thought that their five-pointed star had digested their brains in the same way.

Brkić was lost in thought.

Davor, Sanja, and Julio came back from the hospital two hours later, in the same van. And with the same packing cases. Dad asked what was in them, and one of the Territorials explained that they had taken down the pictures and other works of art in the maternity hospital and sent them to the museum for safe keeping.

Dad wanted to open the cases, count everything, and make an inventory of the transfer, but Julio already had all those papers and the packing cases remained unopened. Julio also asked the commander whether he wanted to take a picture to headquarters.

What for?

To hang it on the wall.

Which one? Two had been destroyed, on the third were the door and a window, and on the fourth a chimney and pipes. Dad still couldn't keep quiet: Were the pictures Julio's private property?

No.

So on what basis was he offering them to others?

The lads were fighters. Defenders. Heroes. They had the right to art. They hadn't been born with rifles. Their eyes needed beauty as well.

Julio carried on embellishing for a few more minutes, until the Defenders left. Then he clapped his hands and in front of the enraged Director opened the packing cases. Then they took out of them a few pictures, mainly reproductions and abstracts, of the kind that institutions buy by the square yard.

However, those pictures were wrapped in the embroidered shirts that had already been grieved over. Thus had the young men from the brown van scattered with yellow fleurs-de-lis done two good deeds in the course of one day: they had taken diapers for the babies and saved the hospital's art works. (I would say that they had saved the people in the hospital from those pictures, but that's not so important.) And the future parents had been to the maternity hospital as well. Here is a condensed sketch of that historic visit, which all told was a small step for the Territorial Defense, but a big one for Sanja and Davor.

When they got there, the first thing they saw were lots of soldiers round the building and in the building itself. Then, all the doctors were standing waiting by reception in the hall. Then the pregnant women, most of them with their personal possessions, were also waiting. The maternity hospital was being evacuated.

As far as Sanja was concerned, the ultrasound apparatus had already been sent to their next destination. They examined her by hand. Everything was fine. And it would continue to be, she should just carry on taking the medicines. (Which she was not taking. She had heard that those medicines made a person shake as though racked by fever.) She should come in a month's time for a checkup. On the way home they were fired at, and it seemed to Sanja as though someone were throwing firecrackers under their wheels.

Mother heaved a sigh of relief, her son had returned safe and unscathed. Dad thanked good fortune, luck, which *favet* (favors) *fatuis* (fools). Dad usually calls luck every mercy shown us by Saibaba.

Saibaba, Sajo, as Mother calls him in her telepathic prayers, has the face of Gandhi, framed in the hairstyle of Jimi Hendrix, and the outfit of an American footballer on the body of a Japanese jockey. His international success, however, is not attributed to his multicultural exterior, but rather to his spiritual principles, with the help of which he creates, out of nothing, by a movement of his hand, the powder called *vibhuti*. For skeptical tourists, instead of powder, he materializes sweets.

Vibhuti has medicinal qualities. It can be drunk like tea, and it can be rubbed onto the third eye, which each of us has between our eyebrows, nose, and forehead. Sai is capable of being in several places at one time, he can walk on water and hover in the air, and many serious witnesses affirm that they've seen it. He has many devotees throughout the world, among all races and on all the continents. They are organized on the principle of sects. They meet in each other's apartments and distribute leaflets and brochures among themselves. (Brkić would have liked that!) Saibabists believe that they live forever, by passing from one life into another, from one body into another. In order to get a better body in the next life, in this one they had to love and sacrifice themselves for others.

We welcome that because it can only be to our advantage.

But Mother smiles wisely, knowing that after a while we others will start to be ashamed and beg for the mercy of soaping our hands in the dishwasher or splashing our feet in the toilet bowl. Mother is running on a different track, Saibaba.

At exactly eight o'clock someone in the city lit a boiler and the power system of the entire country collapsed. We were left without electricity. As usually in such situations, soon, beside our wood-burning stove, a so-called *fiacre*, Mrs. Flintstone appeared.

The loyal reader will allow me to provide an explanation here. It is a question of the concept of refugee. That is, there are two kinds of refugee. The first are people who have moved from one part of the city to another, to friends, relatives, or parents. The others, of whom Mrs. Flintstone is one, moved into the city from its wider surroundings.

They're well connected among themselves and they're usually the first to hear of spacious abandoned apartments and houses. They move into one room, usually the kitchen or the one where the television is, and use the others simply as storage space, for food and other things they receive during the night by way of humanitarian aid. When she doesn't have electricity, the mother of the Flintstones, of whom there are altogether about twenty, comes to our place to finish baking her pies. In their apartment, they have a gas cooker, but they are afraid of gas, so they cook in front of the house. They cook on a stove, when there's power, and on an open fire when there's none. For fuel they use surplus furniture or chop down a tree in no man's land. When, as now, the power cut happens at dusk, or when she needs an oven, she comes to us. On this occasion she appeared in her ceremonial dressing-gown, for going out in, and with a bandage the color of a baking dish round her forehead. Here she received an invitation to this evening's performance.

As will shortly be seen, that performance, which gathered an audience of some thirty people, partly ourselves, partly neighbors, and partly Flintstones, was put on by Davor and Julio. The role of warm-up group at a rock concert was played by Sanja and Sniffy. Although Davor had trained him, and I took him for walks, he still obeyed Sanja best. I wasn't sure whether that was because she fed him or because she had a way with men. For some ten minutes the little Flintstones were thrilled to screaming pitch by Sniffy's artistic act in which he jumped, rolled onto his back, chased his own tail, sang serenades, and, like American presidents, offered every voter first one paw then the other.

In the course of the birth of the idea for the performance itself, I believed that Davor had cheered up after the ultrasound scan. The scene that we had prepared seemed to me really witty. He had found somewhere in the packing cases the uniform of Franz Ferdinand (actually, a copy of it), put it on, sat opposite the audience, and transformed the atrium in an instant into a courtroom. Apart from him, the judges' bench consisted of a stuffed bear and two mannequins from the collection of Sarajevo crafts, two boys in examples of traditional town costume.

The accused, by the name of Zora Princip Seljo (me), a member of the secret organization Young Miljacka (the feminist wing of Young Bosnia) was invited to come forward.

I came forward.

Had I written the following poem: *A butterfly sat on the crown of a flower, It spread its wings over the whole world and set off. Then the meadow was laid bare by a mower, And so the flower's soul at once also let off.*

Yes, I wrote it.

And why had I written it?

It's a lyrical image. The butterfly was afraid of the scythe and flew away, and it seemed to me that the soul of the flower had fluttered off into the sky.

And why had I not written *the soul lifted off*, but *the soul let off*? Did I know what the phrase *let off* meant? (The Flintstones knew as well. Whenever the phrase was mentioned, they split their sides laughing.)

Because of the rhyme.

And why because of the rhyme had I not written a different word, containing the (Bosniak) letter "h"? Because it seems there are some people in our country who don't like the letter "h." We all know who they are.

Who are they?

Those who use this poem to incite people to war. Where is the butterfly sitting?

In the crown of a flower.

In the crown! Why the crown exactly? Since when did flowers have crowns? Everyone knows who has a crown—the Emperor. And what does the butterfly do? It spreads its wings over the whole world. So how big are its wings? No "h" here, wings over the whole world there, a peasant here. Why, for instance, as an example, couldn't it have been *the maiden laid the flowers bare*? Or, for instance, the Austrian army. But a peasant who doesn't like to pronounce the letter "h." Yesterday Young Bosnia, today Young Miljacka, tomorrow Young Danube . . . We know where there's a storm gathering!

Mrs. Flintstone now appeared as a witness. She had a neighbor called Haca who called their dad Asan, instead of Hasan.

Once they realized that the verb "to let off" was not going to recur in the performance, her children turned to mutual nudging, and when they quickly got bored with that as well, they set off to explore the museum. Dad had reckoned with this possibility, however, and had put away and locked up anything they could have damaged. The theatrical production was concluded without applause, comments, or congratulations. Davor collected his props and put them away in front of the perplexed audience just as a traveling salesman would put brochures of fridges back into his briefcase in front of his Eskimo hosts. And I learned that it wasn't enough for something to be really funny in order for someone really to laugh at it.

In the second part of the program, Julio did magic tricks, mostly with cards and coins, but without a hat or doves. At the very end he asked Granny to assist him. Granny refused at first, but under pressure from the small Flintstones she gave way. What Julio had reckoned with happened. Granny stood up, taking her suitcase with her. Davor went up to her and tied a handkerchief over her eyes, probably for effect, because she would have been blind enough if he had only taken off her spectacles.

Mother had used one of the pauses and had already melted away somewhere. Dad was occupied with keeping an eye on the younger generation, whom he evidently didn't trust, although the children were sitting down again, yawning at the magician. Sanja was thinking about the latest symptoms of her potential urinary infection, caused by the *E. coli* bacterium.

Julio asked Gran to sit down on her case. Granny obeyed. Then Julio went up to her and began to take eggs out of her pockets, sleeves, collar, and lapels. When he came to the last egg, he broke it, and out flew a dove. That was effective. The children leapt up to grab the dove, Granddad Flintstone congratulated Julio.

I was the only one who noticed that Davor helped Granny to get up and that as he did so he thrust a suitcase very similar to hers into her hands. She waddled off without noticing the mistake. Davor went out with her suitcase and the other props.

A little later I let him know that I had seen everything.

He told me that it was all a joke.

I told him I didn't believe him.

He told me to mind my own business.

I told him I would, and that I would make a note in my book of how he had robbed his very own Granny. We were interrupted by the telephone. I was faster. It was his Dad, calling from Belgrade. To ask how we were. Where was Davor? Here. Could he speak to him? Here he was.

But Davor refused to take the receiver. I carried on the conversation: Davor was busy right now. Was Davor well? Fine. And Sanja? She was fine, too. Was there any way he could get to talk to Davor? He was tied up at the moment. He hadn't been taken away somewhere? No, he was right here.

Now I was beginning to feel sorry for the man. I thrust the receiver at Davor and moved away. He stood and listened, his chin was trembling, he wanted to answer several times, but he only yawned. I took the receiver from him: Hello, Davor had gone out. Was he alive? Yes, he was fine. Was Mother nearby? Could he speak to her?

Craaackle. The connection was lost. Had there been such a thing as a telephone in his day, Shakespeare would have included this whole scene in *Hamlet*. All in all, this night had not been Davor's day.

■ □ ■ □ ■

CHAPTER FOUR

A satanic device. A well. A little walk through three-way roads. Burnt sugar teeth. Julio's war stories, *The Tangk* and *The Bungker*. Low-flying Beetle.

THERE'S BEEN NO POWER FOR THREE DAYS NON-STOP. WE EXPECTED that Granny would start to wilt without her television like a cactus without sun, but she adopted all the supplies of candles and, with her case on her knees, she embarked on a pageant of patience. Sanja, Davor, Julio, and I sat or stood round her, waiting for her to start drooping so that we could start playing. Granny's cards are the size of matchboxes, and great for arranging on a small suitcase. That was why we were all waiting for them, rather than playing with our own. As soon as card playing had experienced a boom among the lodgers, Julio had got everyone a new pack.

The Flintstone children, the little Flintstones, say that cards are a satanic (devilish) device, because they have images on them and lead to sin. A computer is also a satanic device, they say. They learn that at school. Religious employees, unlike teachers, are exempt from military service.

Nighttime is worst, without light. The candles are being kept for Judgment Day. We have gas lamps, but no gas, we have flashlights, but there are no batteries for them. The only batteries we have are the ones in the Walkman, and Dad is in charge of those. The Walkman is turned on once every eight hours, so we can hear the latest news.

Some people connect a bulb to their car battery, but Dad won't let us do that. Who knows, he might need to start the car the next day, and the battery would be dead. Brkić and Mother made something we call an icon lamp. First water is poured into glasses, half way up, then oil is poured in on top, then a piece of cork wrapped in foil with a hole through the middle is floated on top of that. A piece of shoelace soaked in oil is drawn through the hole and lit. That invention is capable of burning the whole night through, although Mother takes care that this doesn't happen or we might run out of oil. (Or else she's afraid of an explosion. Once the air was full of gas that we tried for ages to find the source of, suspecting each other, while Davor pointed at Sniffy. The gas had the smell of chicken bones, which Sniffy acquires and eats in enormous quantities, and which arrive from all directions, out of thawed deepfreezes. Sniffy profited in another way as well: When we removed the blackout from some of the windows, he was the first to plant himself by them and take charge of the traffic in the street.)

In the name of art, however, after three days, I've begun to write again. I can't reconcile myself to the fact that one bottle of oil could be more important than a work of literature. In the meantime, I read. In the museum courtyard, on a bench, under the aroma of pine trees. I read *Ex ponto* by Ivo Andrić. It was wonderful to discover that he had once been young. Reading good writers and rejoicing in their weak points means being well on the way to becoming a writer. I also read Čapek's *Stories from the Left and Right Pockets*. The deepest pocket is one with a hole in it. (Why did I write that? What did I mean? It sounded wise, but it probably doesn't mean anything.)

My schoolmates had either left or they lived in parts of town that could only be reached by defying my father's ban and over my mother's dead body. My teacher, with whom I would have gladly discussed the problem of war in fiction, was also out of reach. The cinemas were not functioning, the theaters were closed, the television programs, when there was power, cried out for euthanasia. Writing, therefore, was not a matter of choice, it was for me a matter of survival. Had the post been working, maybe I would have written letters. On the other hand, this could be a big letter, and when it's published it will be as though I had sent it to each of my friends.

They would certainly have most liked to read about me, but there was no news there. I was still mistress of my heart. Last night I thought I heard someone playing a musical instrument, then I thought maybe I could also hear a song, finally I couldn't believe that that group of people had sent me an invitation to join them via Mother.

I hadn't accepted the invitation, because I didn't know any of them, I didn't have anything appropriate to wear as a costume, and I didn't know the words of the songs, combative love songs, about war. I would probably have forgotten the whole incident, had I not later heard, when they had long since dispersed, someone plucking the strings of a guitar, as though weaving a story or a dream.

In the leisure time between two shellings, Dad decided to collect in one place all the papers and documents connected with the building of the museum itself and its legal status. He succeeded in establishing that its owner was the Republic, that its building and fittings were financed by Austro-Hungary. But the greatest consequence for us all was the discovery that the museum's specifications included a well with a source of drinkable water. Dad translated some correspondence between the architect and the head office in Vienna, and deduced, with great conviction, that the well was under the paving of the small atrium: It would be good to do a spot of digging. It was only a matter of days before the Chetniks would think of turning off the city's water, as they had the electricity. Who knows, maybe the spring was still active.

Julio and Brkić agreed. Davor shrugged his shoulders. He didn't care whether he carried packing cases with exhibits or dug holes for garbage and wells. So the title of First Spade of the museum smiled on him.

Then one day all morning, there was measuring, drawing, treading every which way, banging on the ground with a pickax, and finally encircling of the edge of the future hole. And the same day all afternoon Julio spat on his palms and Davor struck the first blow with the pick between the bricks. Mother came for Julio, he was needed on the phone, from Belgrade. That was how I overheard what life was like in the town that was dying, and into which chroniclers like Ivo Andrić were prevented by their parents from going: People ran over crossroads. Their necks disappearing between their hunched shoulders. All the shop windows were shattered. The shops were open, but they weren't working, because they had neither goods nor staff. There were just two where you could buy small packets of pepper and the picture book *Little Bairam Shoes*. Bread was sold directly from trucks. The price had stayed the same, but the loaves were not quite half their former size. If someone said in the morning that a sniper had just missed him on some pedestrian crossing, everyone avoided that crossing all day. One-way streets had become three-way. (Both directions and upwards.) Many people only realized that when it was too late.

The famous question asked by fans in Belgrade was who was throwing bombs at the city? They could not believe that it was being done by their brother Serbs. True believers do not believe anything other than what is obviously unbelievable. Like, for example, the fact that the Muslims had fired a million shells at themselves. (And that was obviously unbelievable because the only people who had a million shells at the beginning of the war were the Serbs.) The Belgraders, however, didn't like mathematics, because it was an abstract science and nowhere near as exact as history.

I would add to Julio's report some of my own through-the-window round-the-museum observations, as well as some data from over-a-coffee chatting: The defenders of the city walked among the civilians, mice, basement-dwellers, and other university-educated citizens, armed with compulsory cowboy holsters with pistols in them on one hip, and long hunting or kitchen knives on the other. Their horses were half-trashed requisitioned cars.

There were medicines. The best stocked were the chemists that were never open. Newspapers were sold only by journalists. It was assumed that the articles in them were written by the editors. The market was empty. Once a day people fought each other in a queue for a kilogram of green apples, half-wild pears, a bag of nettles. No one stopped to talk to anyone else. Greetings were exchanged on the move. The best that could happen was that friends, when they shook hands, would make several circles round each other. In the city, apart

from the defenders, who were divided into volunteers and the mobilized, one could also meet men who were not Defenders. They
worked in public utilities, such as the water supply or in the local
authorities or in radio and television. Or else they were pensioners.

Since I've mentioned the Radio, as an institution, Davor had been
on "waiting" since the previous day. (In wartime that was what was
called a technological surplus. Or rather an ideological surplus.
Other people waiting were women with small children. I shall try to
explain this new category of the population. The difference between
the ones waiting and those working lies in the fact that the em-
ployed receive full pay, parcels of supplies, and, what seems the
most important thing, cigarettes, while those waiting get only their
pay. And then it's the smallest sum envisaged by law, after the greatest length of time not envisaged by law. The difference between
those waiting and those who had been fired lay in the fact that those
who had been fired were now somewhere in the hills and from up
there they made no distinction between those who were waiting
and those who had so-called employment duties.) Even before this,
Davor had compared the building of Radio-Television, known as
RTV House, to a beehive in which the new queen bee was selected
from among the old drones, so the new buzzing neither surprised
nor bothered him.

So, this would be the main reason why the drama about the inhabitants of the museum was no longer being recorded. The tape recorder had been returned. Now, like the sword of Damocles over
our heads hung the obligation for Davor to register with a unit of
the Armed Forces. (Somewhat belatedly, I also discovered that the
TO was now called the AF.)
    When Davor said something in Mother's presence that sounded
as though he was himself responsible for his fate, that he had refused to work, Mother was surprised: What had he refused to do?
    To make a documentary drama about one of the leaders of the
city uprising. But Davor was not Walter Scott, and he seriously
doubted that this defender of rights was Robin Hood, as people
were inclined to say. Davor wasn't going to be a balladmonger.

That's to say, he could not create odes to people who were defending the city in order to be able to plunder it more easily.

Had Davor observed that?

What?

People plundering the city?

Every day.

And did he think it was a greater sin to plunder the city or raze it
to the ground?

He was going to ask Mother something: Would she hate herself
less if his father had not abandoned her?

It was a low blow.

Mother bit her lip and went away. Davor felt bad as well. It's not
only because of the bombs that war is hard, but because of the hor-
rible things we say to one another increasingly often. Once I heard
and remembered, I think it was in fact Davor who said it, that we
behave most meanly with those who love us most, because we count
on their forgiving us our meanness.

Sanja was worried about her teeth. She had a biological filling in
one, while the temporary one had been quite washed away. Then
Davor opened his mouth wide and showed the two broken pillars
of his smile, so-called stumps: He had been eating toast, and they
had shattered as though they were made of burnt sugar.

Was he accusing her? Had she demanded that he give her his
milk, eggs, and vitamin tablets?

No. But she certainly needed them more than he did.

But it seemed as though she were to blame for the fact that his
teeth were shattering as though they were made of burnt sugar.
Everyone was doing what they thought she needed and not what
she really needed.

And what did she really need?

Davor to be like he used to be.

Like what? What used he to be like?

Different. He wasn't aggressive, cynical, ironic. (That was true.
Davor had changed.) What did dying children care whose guns
were firing the shells?

The children didn't. But others exploited that, accusing people without proof . . .

What proof? If it were proved that those madmen on the hills had not fired a single shell into the city, would he be able to believe such proof?

Things were hard for him.

Would he be better off somewhere else? In Belgrade?

Somewhere where he wouldn't be killed for thinking differently.

There was a war here. He'd be killed even if he thought the same.

He wasn't a warrior.

She knew that. But there were differences between a warrior and a fighter. He wouldn't have to make war, just let him fight.

Who for? For which flag?

For her and the baby. For diapers.

How?

I didn't hear anything more, they began whispering. I heard the second installment only that afternoon when Dad asked Davor: Was it true?

What?

That he'd been fired?

It was true.

Was he going to sign up today?

Where?

With the Armed Forces?

No. This wasn't his war.

Ecce homo! Whose was it, if not his?

The ones who paved the way for it.

And who were they?

Everyone knew.

Julio got involved as well. Was it perhaps people like him who attacked tanks bare-handed?

Brkić got involved as well and told Julio not to talk nonsense.

Pardon. Julio wasn't talking nonsense. He had photographs, from a newspaper. There, that's a tangk, and there, only you couldn't see too well, was him. It said here, his unit.

Balderdash. (Brkić heard this word for the first time here, and immediately included it among his favorites.)

Julio had even been wounded. He still had a bandage. He knew it was rude, but he would roll up his trouser leg. (He rolled up the left one first, but remembered that all three wounds on that side had healed.) The one from the tangk was on the other leg. (He took off his Jugosport gym shoes, and his Ključ socks, and showed the bruise on his instep.)

Davor was beginning to get annoyed: How did he get that wound?

From an explosion.

A stove had exploded when it fell on his foot!

Pardon!

It was true that there were those who attacked bare-handed, only it had nothing to do with tanks, but warehouses.

Julio frowned. He looked round for help. Davor went on: Where did the stove come from? And the television? The food?

Julio had brought all of that from his house.

The food as well?

The food as well. He had stores.

Three hundred kilos of pepper? Two hundred packets of black-currant blancmange?

Confused by Davor's attack, Julio put his sock into his pocket, and his trainer back onto his bare foot. When Davor mentioned the pepper, he puffed out his chest and said with great dignity to every-one, not looking anyone in particular in the eye, that he was not surprised that a young man, a coward and deserter, was slandering him, but he was surprised that the others permitted it. And he, Julio, had never taken anything from any kind of warehouse. He was not a thief. The three hundred kilos of pepper, and the black-currant blancmange, and the sack of citric acid, and the two sacks of green peppers—he had been given it all.

Given it?

Yes. In exchange. He had given his plane ticket away, and in return got all that.

And he hadn't left in that plane, because he couldn't leave his comrade, Brkić, who was old and ill, with no home or pension. And that comrade said balderdash.

In the end he wiped his nose and eyelashes with his sock, bowed to my Mother, poured a cold glance over Brkić, and went out without a word.

I had read Venyamin Kaverin's book, *In Front of the Mirror*. I decided to stop writing and enter a monastery. Davor often mentioned a place called Hilandar. I would take the spiritual name of Elisaveta and would become a nun. I would read nothing but the Bible and I'd learn it by heart.

This was the natural reaction of crushed vanity. I see, therefore I know I'm envious. Descartes. Instead of being happy that such a book had been written, I was unhappy because I hadn't written it myself.

For two days my brother was someone else. A stranger. *Persona incognita*. He didn't eat, he gave a start every time the telephone rang, every hour he fought for the transistor headphones. Sanja asked him what he was expecting to hear.

He didn't hear the question. I know that people who wear glasses can't hear properly when they take them off. But I didn't know that people couldn't see properly when they covered up their ears. Davor stared without blinking, as though he were in the power of a hypnotist. That was, of course, enough for Sanja to put her nose three degrees of geographical height into the air. For a pregnant woman it was a question of survival whether her husband was capable and willing to notice her at every instant. She stood in front of Davor and repeated her question, with just her lips and no voice.

Davor removed the headphones from his ears: He hadn't understood what she was asking.

If he were interested, he would have understood, she said, and then turned and walked away.

But an invisible string drew Davor after her, tore him away from the transistor and pulled him out of the room. Comparison: He had been flying on a kite on the waves of Radio Belgrade, and then a magpie came along, crapped on his kite in flight, and obliged him to make a forced landing.

How did I know he had been listening to Radio Belgrade? Simple, he had not been frowning. When he listens to Sarajevo, it's as though he were sitting on a tub of sour cabbage. Mother's face, when she hears recipes for dishes made with meat. Dad's, when he stumbles on bush radio. (Serbian hill radio, broadcasting from Pale. In Belgrade, they now talk about citizens of Pale. That was like Mother saying seaweed with pork, or Brkić cherry cognac. But from someone who's capable of saying meat pie with meat, nothing should surprise us.) When Granny listens to the radio, she has an expression as though there's something very smelly in front of her. But she has that expression when she's not listening to the radio as well. Brkić never follows the news, while Julio knows it before it's broadcast.

The first of the ten gynecological commandments to Sanja is that she must not bend down. When Davor followed her into their room, she was already kneeling combing the tassels. Tassels are the decorative edge of rugs. As a result of being walked on, predominantly by Davor, who drags his feet along the floor, the tassels get crooked, bent, tangled, and in every possible way defy the order which Sanja's degree in architectural engineering expects of them.

Sanja decided to break the gynecological commandments every time she felt like screaming, without anyone other than Davor hearing her. He, of course, knelt down immediately, took the comb from her and started combing the rug: What made her do this all of a sudden?

Why not?

Because she shouldn't.

Who cared what happened to her?

Davor.

He was lying. Everyone was lying. It would be best if they parted. She and Davor could never be a couple.

They were a couple.

No, they weren't. She would like to live with him, but not with his family. As long as they were all together, he would always be his mother's son first and foremost, and only after that her husband.

I heard Davor whispering. I call that tone his priestly approach. Then I heard her: Where could they run away to?

Her brother, in Australia.

How?

He'd find a way. They'd bribe someone. The planes that flew aid in went out empty.

What about visas? And hard currency? What would they bribe anyone with? A ten-deutsche mark note? Besides, in her condition she was not allowed to fly.

Then they'd get onto one of the convoys.

They didn't take young men. The convoys went through Serbian territory. And even if they were allowed to leave the city, the Serbs would mobilize him at the first barricade.

No, they wouldn't. He'd explain . . .

What? That he was on their side? That he approved of their destroying the city? She hardly recognized him anymore. He had completely changed. He was becoming irrational. A coward. It was tough for others as well. He was the head of the family. He was going to be a father. He should just face facts.

He couldn't. It was beyond him. He couldn't take that oath. He couldn't wear that uniform.

Why not?

Because it was stupid. He hadn't chosen to be a Serb, he didn't feel he was, but it was stupid to die like a *shehid*. (That was a new word. I asked what it meant. Julio compared it to national heroes, someone who lost his life in war, and after the war got a pension, a street named after him, and a statue. He had missed the opportunity in that last war. Brkić had saved his life. Mother reproached Julio for scoffing at such things, while Dad explained that *shehids* were fighters who died defending their faith, their family, and their homes.)

Sanja didn't understand Davor. Why be afraid in advance? None of that need happen. Besides, maybe they'd give him his job back.

They were coming down. I turned away so that they didn't catch me in the function of omniscient narrator and I bumped into Julio and Granny. They had gone to look for the transistor. Granny was holding Julio's arm. She shuffled along, dragging her feet on the stone floor. I heard him several times telling Granny the day's events. I'll write down some of Julio's war stories tomorrow.

The first of Julio's war stories: *The Bungker*
High Command calls me and asks if I'd be able to destroy a bungker. Yes, I can do that. But only if they gives me infra-red goggles and a so-called nitroglycerine gun. OK. I looks through the binoculars, in front of the bungker one guard's carving the figure of Vuk Karadžić onto a *gusle,* another's eating bean stew and spitting wood splinters in one direction and uncooked beans in the other, while the third's sticking together a matchstick model of Hilandar. I tells my two companions to find a garbage Dumpster with wheels that works. Then I gets into the Dumpster, pulls down the lid and knocks three times. The lads push me to the middle of the crossroads and go back. Silence. Night. I lifts the lid a bit and looks: the one with the *gusle* didn't have enough wood, all there is of the whole of Vuk Karadžić is his wooden leg, so now he's making it into a chibouk. They've driven the one eating beans away so he won't stink them out, the third's blowing on the glue to make it dry. I puts on the IR goggles, they barely penetrate the bungker, Smederevo-made armature. In the bungker is the high command. Sprinkled with stars like the Milky Way. Two are standing over a map, the others are watching a porn movie and nudging each other. I drags myself closer, wipes the goggles, no use, I can't see what the film is. The two by the map take felt-tip pens, one yellow and one blue, and draw. Then they, too, starts staring at the television. I drags myself still closer, strains my eyes as far as I can, I can see a dark screen, with just a few little spots moving left and right. One green, one red, one lilac. Maybe it isn't a porn movie, maybe it's a computer and they're preparing a general attack on Sarajevo. I moves a little closer. It is a porn movie. And the colors I can see are condoms. Fluorescent. The blue one is chasing the white, the white the red, while the generals are urging them to make a tricolor. Until one of them takes a look at the map. And there the yellow and blue are merging, and everything's beginning to look green. Alarm! Then I takes aim, fires, and inertia drives the Dumpster backwards and I don't see whether I've hit them. Dash to the HQ, for the news. Bravo! Right in the middle of the bungker. Not a stone's standing. I goes back the next day for a second look, and I can't believe my eyes: the grass round about is still smoking, but during the night they've built another identical concrete bungker in the same place. They've even inscribed AHQ just where it had been the previous day.

This is the kind of story Julio tells Granny, but she's never the only listener. Either I'm there, or several younger representatives of the Flintstone dynasty. Whether he made them up himself, or only heard them from someone else, or remembered them from the previous war, I don't know. But I'll try to write down one or two more.

Davor has read my manuscript. I know that because he made a note in the margin that women aren't allowed in Hilandar. I'd wanted to give it to him to read, in any case, but just then I was furious. What gave him the right?! That's why I decided to write something that I had thought of leaving out.

One of the greatest problems in his marriage is the opening in his body a little above the place where his legs meet at the back. When he thinks that no one is looking, he scratches that place, gazing at a fixed point as though he were meditating. He does it the same way that people pick their noses, or scrape young dandruff from the top of their heads.

This habit of his drives Sanja wild. What else drives her wild? His scratching his toes before falling asleep. To be accurate, absolutely precise, his scratching between his toes. What drives Mother wild? Granny's silent farting . . .

Maybe this will seem excessive to some, but I have not permitted myself to fall in love or think of marriage precisely because of my fear of these or similar examples which provoke profound revulsion in me. I can barely manage my own body.

The Territorial, who somebody said looked like Tom Cruise, helped Julio carry various boxes and packing cases in and out. In a break, he came into the porter's lodge and asked me what I was writing. Notes in the daily log book, was what I replied. Why hadn't I told him the truth? Because it's quite enough that he should laugh with his fellow fighters over my short-sight, there's no need for him also to laugh at my preoccupation with writing a diary-novel-chronicle.

However, Julio had already told him what I was writing. (How did Julio know?) He'd like to read it. He couldn't was my reply. I was furious, and I went away so that no one should laugh at that as well. What gave him the right to come in, to interrupt me, to interrogate me, wink and smile, as though I had nothing else to do apart from pretending to write and waiting for him to come in and ask me what I was writing. I was writing texts for love ballads with a war theme!

Investigating the source of little bouquets of chard and bunches of parsley on the market tables, Dad and Julio, independently of one another, had discovered that inside the Serbian ring of steel round the city there were households occupied with agriculture and growing vegetables. All of them, for the most part Croatian, were on the side of Sarajevo opposite us, in the villages of Stup and Azići.

Dad remembered that there were people he knew there, Julio got hold of gas for the car and a car, and we all made a list: eggs, carrots, new potatoes and onions, chard, beetroot . . .

Azići and Stup, if I had understood correctly and processed the data accessible to me, had the function of a little window in a prison cell. People went out through them, and goods came in, you paid good money for everything—freedom and cigarettes—with the same currency.

They wouldn't allow Davor, who offered to drive, to go with them, because three was too many, the road was dangerous: The Beetle would have to fly low past the barrels of Serbian anti-aircraft guns. At the same time they wouldn't be able to get up any speed, because every few hundred yards local police or the army carried out detailed searches of vehicles, people, and documents.

The send-off itself was touching. Mother put a bit of *vibhuti* on the Beetle's brow, Granny asked Julio to buy her a box of Kraš chocolates, Sanja brushed the dust off the bulletproof vests Dad and Julio had forced themselves into, Davor gave final instructions for the part of the road he knew, Sniffy raised his left hind leg and peed on the right rear tire. Brkić stayed in the porter's lodge, in order not to bash Julio on the helmet with a spade. (Julio had found that helmet, German, from the last war, with still visible SS lightning bolts on one side, in the collection of exhibits from the National Liberation War and Revolution.)

Then the brave pilots rolled away over the cobbles.

Mother spent the next few hours rinsing flour and transcendentally meditating. Granny inquired of her cards whether to eat the caramels in the chocolate box first or to leave them to last. Sanja embroidered and crocheted a new collection of little pillows for pins which could be worn like lapel badges or pendants. Davor was finishing the fence round the well, in which there most probably never would be water, apart from in the mud and silt on the bottom, and which we would, most probably, use as a fridge.

The Beetle stopped outside the museum approximately three hours later. Sniffy heard the engine and recognized it and alerted the rest of us. No one had stopped Dad and Julio, either on the way there or on the way back, no one had shot at them or after them, only as they entered Stup, the Sarajevo San Marino, they had to pass through customs formalities. And then when they saw Julio under the helmet, it all turned into a joke and the back seat of the car was jam-packed with greens and eggs.

So the journey was more than worthwhile. We would have carrots and chard until the end of the war, as long as it didn't last more than two years, and if someone stopped Granny sharpening her false teeth on carrots. We saw the chocolates, sixteen quarter-pound boxes, only as a vision. Sniffy raised his right hind leg and peed on Julio's left trouser leg.

CHAPTER FIVE

Brkić hangs out flags. *Fata viam invenient.* A *hamam* for brainwashing.
A book-sized brown bag. A snow-storm rages and in it Korchagin.
Archangels' tracks.

THE GREATEST LOSERS IN THIS WAR, AFTER US YOUNG PEOPLE, WHO
have lost the coming thirty years, are the old people, who have lost
the preceding fifty. That's why Brkić decided to leave the city. On
several occasions he formulated his idea of doing so by balloon. I
shall describe it here in a shortened version.

What stimulated him was the discovery of flags in the cellar. Piles
of flags. Some of them belonged to the museum, and were intended
for public display on holidays. Another pile, considerably larger,
was there by chance: Dad had done someone a favor and kept them
safe in his store. A third pile also belonged to the museum, they
were the flags of the Partizan units, which, in the last war, partici-
pated in the action of liberating Sarajevo. Since tricolors with five-
pointed stars had subsequently gone out of fashion, the bales of
bound flags had begun to fill with dust instead of wind.

Brkić's idea further relied on the Singer sewing machine (the one
Danilo Kiš drew in his novel *Garden, Ashes*), Julio's gas cylinders,
and ropes from the Collection of Sarajevo Crafts.

I was present when he asked Sanja whether they had studied
math in her course.

At that moment she was kneeling, pushing the inquisitive Sniffy
away with one hand, and with the other brushing the rug, and collecting his freshly shed hairs. The best way of preventing their

dispersal throughout the museum was to catch them in flight or just as they landed: Yes, they had studied math.

Would she be able to calculate something for him?

What?

Could one make a balloon out of flags?

As in everything else, Sanja was thorough. Thanks to her, the problem acquired a definitive mathematical form, in the shape of a bunch of Greek letters pinned to a fractional line. Of the units known to me, the following were mentioned: squared and cubed yards, pounds, seconds, newtons, joules, moles, kelvins . . . The balloon would rise if the air in it were heated. (Pressure and specific density of air.) The balloon would not rise if it were too heavy. (Pressure, gravitation, load weight, canvas, basket . . .) The balloon would rise if it were large enough and hot enough. (Capacity of the ball, energy.) It would not rise if the loss of heat were great. Flags, two hundred flags (surface of the ball), would let air out, but it could be additionally heated. (One cylinder for blowing up the balloon and heating the air, another for topping up and steering the balloon.) All in all, difficult, dangerous, risky, impossible.

Enough for Brkić not to give up.

Mother asked whether there weren't another way?

No. A former Partizan was not about to fill in some Ustasha or Chetnik questionnaires, in order to travel with women and children.

Dad offered to try to sort it without questionnaires.

Did the Director mind about the flags?

No, but it could all look rather suspicious to some people.

Was the Director frightened?

No, but the police . . .

That was Brkić's problem.

In the end Dad gave the flags, and rope, and the sewing machine, Mother and Sanja took it in turns to sew, Sanja did the smaller pieces, which Mother then joined together. Julio took it on himself to concoct a burner, Brkić and Davor would see what could be used to improvise a basket.

————————

Mrs. Flintstone, of whom it could be said that she came into the category of women who spent their youth in a state of pregnancy, was a guest in our residence today. She didn't, of course, come because she loves us, but to roast coffee on our fire. Like most other things, she did this in a traditional way, several hundred years old, the so-called Siemens-Martin *shish*-procedure. A *shish* is a can stuck onto a long stick. The can has a little door, which is closed when it is filled with raw coffee beans. The can is shaken in the fire and heated, until, on the basis of the aroma, it's decided that the coffee is properly roasted.

That aroma brought not only me but also Sanja, Davor, and Brkić into the kitchen. Half-joking, half-sorrowfully, Mother mentioned the fact that we had been drinking teas for two days now. That was for my benefit, because Mother can do without coffee. Besides, since we've been teetotal (tea-drinkers), she isn't left out.

Brkić then asked what had happened to the sack with Brazil written on it.

Mother shrugged her shoulders: Julio had taken it away.

How?

The way he brought it. On his back.

One of the strange things connected with my homeland is economics, or more exactly the traffic of goods. On the whole there is none, and everyone regrets that there isn't, but when people talk about it, they talk about cardboard boxes, packets, trailers. It seems that one of the local laws of economics is that the less there is of an article, the larger the units of measure in which it is mentioned. Like coffee. We have been drinking tea for two days, and Julio brings in and carries out sacks. (Units for measuring coffee: *fildžan, džezva*, pan, spoon, mill, eight ounces, one pound, a sack, a trailer, a boat.) We could thank him and Mother for the fact that our supplies of vegetables for the next two years had been reduced to an amount barely sufficient for a month. Julio had exchanged a fair amount for heaven-knows-what, while Mother would probably be able to explain in connection with the carrots and the neighboring children why, one afternoon sucking, scraping, munching, and crunching could be heard from all the houses round the museum.

I've got it! Julio exchanged the vegetables for a portable stove, a godsend for making coffee, saving fuel and time. Hand on heart, the stove was the loveliest I'd ever seen. But, when we wanted to try it, it turned out that it was not intended for us, but for Sanja's employer. (Sanja does not embroider little pillow-badges anymore, but crochets and sews bed linen, tablecloths, and curtains for model furniture for dolls. Her colleague from her student days, the aforementioned employer, had the idea of offering this handmade furniture to the Western market. He pays so well, that envy prevents me from describing all the beauty of the little flowers and pieces of lace that emerge from Sanja's fingertips.)

Description of Mrs. Flintstone:
   She always wears a plush housecoat of tiger or leopard fur. Under her dressing gown, or as we say in the Bosnian language, *schlafrok*, Adidas gym shoes with four white lines (stripes) on them peek out. Under the gym shoes are nylon stockings. The nylon stockings are then drawn into woollen socks, so-called knitted slippers, and the whole lot is then squashed into mules with fur on them, which, for interneighborly flights are shoved into old men's shoes.
   Mrs. Flintstone talks approximately like this: give me a little water, blessyou; eh, thanks, godsaveyou; godgrant the chemist be open nonstop; very handy, *mashalla;* it wasn't me, on my soul; I didn't, godstrikemedead!
   She said this last after Mother complained that our canister had disappeared. (The tanker comes once a day. All citizens, including those who have wells in their yards, but who don't have water in their wells, and who gravitate to our pipeline catchment area, leave their canisters on the pavement, in the order they arrived. When the tanker comes, everyone rushes out of their houses, picks up their canisters and starts shoving to ensure no one begins filling up out of turn. In that pushing and shoving, half the water from the tanker gets spilt. Half is poured into several fifteen-gallon barrels. Half is poured through the gate into the yards of prominent people. And half is kept by the driver for his house. How many of those halves make a whole? Not enough, as may be concluded from the fact that after the arrival of the tanker half the canisters from the queue go empty to look for water somewhere else. Dad, who, as a historian is always a step ahead of his times, has already acquired the habit of

going to meetings in the Ministry, carrying a gallon canister instead of a briefcase. *Per kanistra ad astra.*)

However, Mrs. Flintstone had not taken our canister, as she had not taken anything of what she now had, after the Chetniks had driven her out with nothing whatever. While she was grinding her coffee, she did a bit of grinding of us as well. We heard what she was cooking for lunch, that she had thought that a microwave oven was a "fortable" television set, that in their new apartment she had found a typewriter with a Cyrillic keyboard. Her children were sick, one had dried up, and was immured to medicines, while the other had gone for the runs . . .

Mrs. Flintstone wouldn't shove herself up the tanker's arse even if someone drove her with a pistol. Thank god her Junuz went with the van to fetch their water. And why didn't her Director ask for a van for the museum?

Because they didn't need one.

What about wood, what did they burn?

There was still a bit of coal in the cellar.

Handy! Her Junuz had four yards up there at his post, and he'd bring it. She'd heard the Director's a doctor?

Yes.

Fine, *mashalla*. And what about that dried-up one of hers?

He was a doctor of historical science.

Ah well!

Not knowing the real application of the stove-beauty, Mother put a coffeepot on top of it, shoved cardboard and chippings into it, and lit it. The stove melted. Brkić's favorite saying: Everything's possible, apart from a wooden furnace, now had to be adjusted: A tin furnace wasn't much use, either.

Fata (real name Mrs. Flintstone) doesn't come round to our place more than seventy times a day. When Sniffy barks at the sound of her footsteps, Dad says *Fata viam invenient* (the Fates are knocking at the door) and goes off to find something to do in another place.

Fata arrives in the same way every time: she comes in, puffs, sits down, puffs, waves her hand in front of her face like a fan, puffs, and then we learn of the terrible thing that has befallen her. Once, while there was still power, the washing machine emptied all its water into the toilet bowl on which she was sitting. It completely, if you'll excuse me . . . sluiced her. Or, she had just put shampoo on her hair, and the water went off. Or, she pulled off a sheet of toilet paper, the whole roll unwound.

Just before the end of a hot spell, as a result of a temporal miscalculation, Dad came back. Mrs. Flintstone now knew that he was a doctor of history. I presume that she wanted to make an impression, or to be witty, when she asked whether, byAllah, there had ever been such bestial shelling of a city.

Dad didn't know whether anything like this had been recorded.

Anti-aircraft guns were now active in the marginal areas, and it had also been observed that the Aggressor was regrouping material and technical staff, as well as bringing in fresh personnel, but our lines were impenetrable and firm and the Aggressor would not succeed in realizing his criminal aims.

Dad remembered that he hadn't closed the window. I took advantage of his departure myself.

I must observe that certain changes may be seen on Dad.

First, he, too, has acquired accreditation. He wears it on his lapel. That's an external mark of change. The inner change, far more significant, consists in the following: A few days ago he introduced a compulsory watch in the porter's lodge. *Dictum factum.* We keep watch with a notebook in which it is our job to write down all our observations. We are also obliged to have with us, in case of fire or ransack, all the keys to all the rooms. No one is permitted to take anything out of the museum without his permission. Once a day, after supper, Dad reads extracts from the daily newspaper. This evening, after an unexpected lull of several days, the conflict had broken out again. Davor refused to listen to those articles being read.

Dad was surprised, it was courageous to take a stand. However, what was such a brave young man doing here? If he were stationed somewhere, rifle in hand, he would not have to listen.

What, actually, did Dad want?

Davor to sign up for the army.

He had done that once. And served his time.

If he intended to go on hiding in the museum, then let him in future restrain his reactions.

Davor intended to go on hiding in the museum, but this was no longer a museum.

What was it then?

A *hamam* (Turkish bath) in which brainwashing was carried out by reading newspapers.

Better that than a fifth-column hotbed. It was sad that a radio journalist should approve of what was going on.

He didn't approve.

Silence was approval!

Fortunately, Sanja clutched her stomach and groaned, and we all leapt up so that the birth should not surprise us at table. The end of the quarrel was left for one of the subsequent installments of the series *The bald tear their hair out*.

The birth, of course, was not yet on the horizon. I knew that and was able to observe the whole scene from the height of my objectivity. Dad, Davor, and Brkić took Sanja to her room. Granny stayed to collect the leftovers from their plates, Julio helped Mother to clear the table, and then sat down and rolled a cigarette out of the article Dad had marked.

That same evening I seized the opportunity to mention Davor's gullibility with respect to his wife. Because the twenty-ninth attack of premature birth had ended with him holding her hand and making mini-sandwiches, so-called bitelets, which, in addition to all their other qualities, could be eaten while lying in bed. (When she was full or pleased for some other reason, Sanja began to speak in the diminutive.)

He replied that anyone who had been bitten by a snake was afraid of lizards.

I remembered that the two of them had already been through a pregnancy, and that it had ended badly, but nevertheless . . .

Following my previous note, Davor is now sitting at the table, listening to Dad reading, and making little balls of breadcrumbs. And today will be remembered for the fact that we got our long expected and awaited humanitarian aid.

This consists of a certain quantity of food with which the civilized world wishes to feed the starving Sarajevans. Feed them is perhaps a bit of an exaggeration. This reminds me of the fairytale about Ivica and Marica. I think that the aim of the world is to keep us alive, so that, when the war is over, we will be able once again to take out loans from it and buy whatever will be indispensably unnecessary.

For me the most interesting thing of all that we are given is the so-called lunch packets. They are packed in brown paper bags the size of a book (but that doesn't make them unpopular with the people). The bags contain two or three boxes the size of a volume of poems. In the boxes there are brown bags the size of savings-account books and in them, finally, say, a ham omelet. In the book-sized bag, in addition to the cardboard boxes, there are also little brown bags of fruit-juice or cocoa in powder form, and peanut butter or cheese. And finally, one brown rustling bag, in which there are, no one will believe me who hasn't seen it with his own eyes: matches, chewing gum, hot sauce, salt, sugar, coffee, coffee-creamer, a spoon, sweets, a freshening-up tissue, toilet paper.

All in all, more packaging than food. You are worn out unpacking it all. What you see in front of you is a heap of bags, boxes, little bags, pieces of paper, you think there's going to be all sorts. But, in fact, what there is is a book-sized bag. Brown.

The aid is distributed to each municipality, and then to each member of the household. For instance, for one person (me, let's say): 170 grams of peas, 400 grams of cheese, half a kilo of rice, half a liter of oil. In determining the quantities, account is taken of the packing, so that everything has to be cut, weighed, and poured out. When you finally reach the end, you see that the number of calories expended in the course of receiving the food is equal to the number of calories the food contains. (When I read this to Brkić, he said bravo, I'd make a good communist.)

That same afternoon Mrs. Flintstone came round to ask whether we would swap. She had been given food packets with pork in them, and her Junuz didn't eat it. We couldn't help her, our brown bags also had pork and ham written on them. A conversation ensued about the impudence of the western world. Them and their aid. They didn't send what we needed, just what they didn't need.

Julio rebelled. He needed everything in the packet. Even the condoms. They demonstrated that the Americans intended to make Bosnia a condominium.

Mrs. Flintstone hadn't had any of those in her packet.

They must have given her children's packets then.

Brkić to Davor: There's no need to deceive people who can be helped to deceive themselves. I remembered this from a conversation the two of them were having about art and direction. It was the evening following the theater performance. Davor had come to congratulate Brkić. The reader remembers: Julio and Davor produced a performance and exchanged Granny's suitcase. They needed time to do it, because in his nervousness Julio kept dropping the skeleton key. Finally he lifted the lid. And they saw in it everything that they had themselves put into it. Julio was the first to realize what had happened: Brkić had somehow worked out what they were up to and had changed the suitcases over earlier. They had had the right case in their hands the whole evening and gave it back closed and untouched.

On his barge, Brkić (and Julio, when he was in the country) had been friendly with actors and Bohemians. That barge, as far as I can deduce from their stories, was a kind of private pub. Brkić worked for the Politika printing press and there he published special issues of the newspaper, with news with which he began his jokes. (News: the nationalization of hard-currency savings, a special tax on the possession of Moskvich cars, the banning of a book, a false obituary—the reader with imagination may conclude what kind of thing could emerge from such plots in such company.) He was also inclined to teach actors to present themselves falsely and thus, as lovers or undivorced wives, to cause chaos in many hidebound marriages.

Brkić made the following observations to Davor on his job as director: First, writers make gods of people, and directors make them idiots. Second, directors are like lichen on a tree, the greener they are, the more quickly the tree withers. When he reads a book, he doesn't see either the book or the words, but a raging snowstorm and in it Korchagin. But when he saw it in the theater, there was no snow, and no Russia . . .

Brkić wasn't usually so talkative, but when brandy was being distilled, then his simple sentences arranged themselves of their own accord into complex ones.

The distilling of brandy takes place in the atrium, on an improvised apparatus, which in addition to a pressure cooker (so-called prestige), and long copper pipes, relies on Brkić's lengthy experience. The raw materials are water and sugar, enriched with raisins and prunes, and in exceptional circumstances freshly picked crushed fruit: mulberries, cherries, rotten apples, and plums regardless of their degree of ripeness.

The Partizans set about distilling the brandy after they had drunk all the supplies of medicinal alcohol. Julio had found this in the first-aid packs, which Dad had found in the civil defense warehouse, where Julio had also found two hundred sterile needles for single-use syringes.

He intended them for one of the strangest trophies in his commercial activity. Two drug addicts brought into the museum a quarter of a yard of asphalt with the prints of two shoes in it. Left and right. They belonged, legend had it, to the Sarajevan assassin of the Austrian Emperor, Gavrilo Princip. The asphalt had been planted into the pavement in front of the Young Bosnia museum, from where at the beginning of this war national fury had uprooted it and flung it into the Miljacka River, from where it had been dragged out again by addicts' intuition.

Julio offered Dad Gavrilo's footprints, but Dad didn't know what to do with them. And he had the shoes somewhere among his exhibits, so, when an appropriate time came, a new print could be made. Julio had no choice but to sell the piece of asphalt to Unprofor soldiers. The tall, blonde, and broad officers who smelled of after-shave and chewing gum, first wanted to buy a *stećak*. But when Dad refused to listen to Julio, the archangel's shoes were exchanged for a box of goods from the duty-free shop at the airport. Among many colorful items, I saw a jar of Nescafé.

The blue-helmets took their souvenir away in a white bulletproof Land Rover, the windows of which, small and thick, reminded one of the eyes of a white-headed vulture. The only subject on which Dad and Davor agree is their anger with the blue-helmets. Dad compares them to a priest standing in front of the executioner at the execution of the innocent, while Davor sees in them a doctor summoned to confirm death, rather than to prescribe medicines.

I feel in their presence like a llama in the zoo. Let them take this as my way of spitting at them.

■ □ ■ □ ■

CHAPTER SIX

Mother-of-darknesses. Some observations about housing policy in the city. Paper with ciphers. *Angtenna*. *Umbra* again. Sniffy goes to war. Ping and Li Ping.

THERE HASN'T BEEN POWER OR WATER FOR DAYS, AND, IN ALL probability, that is becoming Sarajevo's trademark. We brush our teeth and wash ourselves with one glass of water. Then we use that water to wash our feet. (In Mother's religion kissing other people's feet is one of the paths of spiritual advancement. The guru who first had that idea was certainly not thinking of Julio's feet, from which he never removes his socks, so there's no way they can get dirty. Joke. On the contrary, Julio changes his socks every day. He throws the old ones away and takes new ones out of one of the three sacks which a business friend left him to look after.)

But the worst is the dark. There's no music, there's no television, there's no light for reading. I wanted to write on the cover of this notebook *Sine sole sileo* (Without sun I am silent), as it says under the sundial in the atrium, but then I opted for defiance and I'm writing this beside the *kandilo*.

Dark. Superdark. Mother-of-darknesses. We stumble, bump into mirrors, trip on rugs, knock into trunks. There seem to be none of those terrible nighttime bombardments anymore, so we no longer go down to the cellar. But, things are harder for us now that they're easier. Because, when the power suddenly came on, we didn't know what to do first. Mother made bread, we turned on the washing machine, cassette player, all the lights, and then the power went off. Mother sat in despair in front of the washing machine, looked at the light bulb, and wondered whether to take the washing out of the drum or to leave it to see if it would decide of its own accord whether first to activate itself (agitate itself, Mrs. Flintstone), or start smelling. Soon His Excellency the transistor announced that the power transmission line had been destroyed again. Then, for the nth time, Dad was scandalized and furious at the cruelty of those who were attacking the city. Davor, for the nth time, at the corruption of these here.

Who?

The police, for instance.

Could Davor be thinking that we were destroying our transmission lines ourselves?

There's no need for the transmission line to be destroyed for there to be no power.

But why, in the name of God, who in the city would that benefit?

The Mafia. They don't need power. They have generators (Mrs. Flintstone, a generateror!), radio stations, batteries, accumulators.

Dad didn't understand Davor. Why didn't he explain who in the city benefited from the fact that the museum had not had any power for who knows how many days now?

He'd explain. Without power there was no television. There was no actual news from the ground. Nothing but rumors. Who did that suit? Those who were losing the war, so that they could complain and justify themselves. Without power there were no freezers. Who did that suit? The person who stored stocks of meat and vegetables to sell, who had undertaken to distribute the food arriving in the city. Without power there was no heat. Who did that suit? The person who would be selling coal and wood come the winter . . . All right, says Brkić. There is a Sicilian proverb: You have to see who damage benefits!

Davor was ripe for a lunatic asylum. What spoke out of him was not reason but paranoia. Why would the independent, sovereign, and internationally recognized state plunder its citizens in that way?

Because that was the only way an independent, sovereign, and internationally recognized state could settle its obligations.

I listened to them, and I didn't understand anything. Was nothing really as it logically ought to be? This was all crazy, but so was I. As

Sanja said on one occasion: No one here is normal anymore, it's just as well there's no one to tell us so. And you can't do it from here.

The political situation has postponed for a long time the possibility of abandoning the city. The Serbs of all races, faiths, and nations are militarily the most powerful. Three hundred thousand inhabitants are being fried in the bottom of the pan called Sarajevo.

From somewhere Brkić acquired two baskets of ripe black mulberries. He went to prepare the distillery and by the time he came back, half of one basket had evaporated. Granny hadn't a clue what had happened. She was blue around the lips and up to her elbows. She pretended she didn't understand what Brkić was talking about and carried on reading her newspapers. The newspapers were children's magazines and Politika from Belgrade from a time before I was born. Julio had found them, in Fata's cellar, and she was more afraid of the Cyrillic script they were printed in than eviction.

Mrs. Flintstone entered the museum faster than sound. (Otherwise we hear her first and only later see her.) She'd been with her children to check on their other apartment, in a tower block, a three-room attic apartment, and there on her own door she had found a foreign padlock. Bang on the door, no one comes out, ring, there's no power. Then she pries off the padlock, and a creature comes up, and then there are two, one all la-di-da, and the other just as bad. One yells from halfway up the stairs: Ha! What're they doing in her apartment? And where does it say that it's hers? It doesn't say anywhere, but there was a padlock. There'd been a padlock before, too. And someone had kicked that lock open. It wasn't someone, but her Junuz.

I made a note of this conversation just as an introduction to publishing the results of my investigation into housing policy in Sarajevo during the war. I'm publishing those results here under the title: Some observations in connection with housing policy in Sarajevo during the war.

First hypothesis: With the outbreak of war many citizens abandon Sarajevo. Many apartments are left empty.

Second hypothesis: Serbossor (Serbian aggressor, auth. abbrev.) begins advance toward the city, on account of which many citizens abandon the villages around the city and go down into the city, where they move into the abandoned apartments of the first thesis.

Third hypothesis: All the displaced settlers are in contact. It is usual for several related families to occupy all the empty apartments in one building. This is how the periphery moved into the center, the village into the city. When the telephones were cut off, they continued to call to one another. When the power went off, they began burning furniture. When the drains in the tower blocks became blocked, they started throwing their garbage out of the windows. When the power went off, they turned on generators and accumulators. When the televisions went silent, they switched on the cassette players. They will survive. Natural selection is on their side. They will be victorious. If not over those stronger than them, then certainly over those weaker.

The Flintstone family, without Junuz, whom none of us, apart from Julio, had yet met, often spent the night in our cellar. With every crashing shell, the mater familias jumped on her taboret (a little wooden stool the size of a box of matches, which she evacuates everywhere with her) and says: DearMother, what's that thundering? That was why every evening visit of hers made us nervous. Especially Dad, who had to keep watch over and above his turn, together with Brkić, because we all found it awkward to ask her to keep her children in one place. Perhaps because we felt that we would be asking her the impossible. I think that not all of those children are hers, a few of them are borrowed, although it would not have been surprising in her case if she had given birth to them at intervals of six months.

However, everything has its brighter side. After the first night in the cellar, she and her elder daughters cleaned the cellar thoroughly and turned it into a civilized overnight space. But that meant that we were all obliged to leave our shoes outside the door.

In the course of my watch, I had a visit from Julio's apprentice, the Territorial who wants to read my novel-chronicle, the young man they told he looks like Tom Cruise: Was I ever going to come to the headquarters? Julio could bring me. They sat there at night, even after the curfew, playing music. I didn't have time, went my reply. Julio had told him that I had been asking who it was playing the guitar the other night. What kind of music did I listen to? None, we have no power, went my reply.

I found Julio in the cellar. He was just finishing counting German coins, which no one accepted anymore, but he collected them, because one day their price would soar. I asked him in future not to go around the headquarters telling everyone what I was doing or writing in the museum, and whose names and guitar-playing I was interested in. He, however, correctly interpreted my feigned revolt and replied that he had not said anything to anyone, apart from the boy I was interested in. His name was Mirza.

After he'd finished making the wall round the well, out of bricks and concrete blocks donated by the neighborhood as their investment in the well, in the hope that the mud would clear, Davor was digging again. This time in the garden, a hole for burying burned garbage. The hole didn't have to be deep, because we barely produced any garbage anymore, everything that could be burned was used to boil coffee and heat food.

I have to admit that Davor is fair. He shares all the heavier work with Dad or does it himself, in his spare time, when he's not occupied with his regular marital duties. Instead of listing and describing them, I shall make a note of some of Julio's dreams.

Once he dreamed about a beach. Men were running into the ocean with surfboards, while Davor had an ironing board. Then Davor was a railway worker, waving a hot iron. Or a fire: Dad and Brkić were putting out the fire with foam apparatus, while Davor was fanning the flames with a vacuum cleaner. He was playing Sanja a serenade under her window, but instead of a guitar, he was holding a carpet beater.

Our rubbish hole is nicer and tidier than other people's, but other people's rubbish is nicer and richer than ours.

But then Dad stood up and asked us to listen to him carefully. He was holding a sheet torn out of a notebook.

We knew that there was such a thing as the fifth column. It could be anywhere. Even in the museum. And he had found something! What was this?

Julio took the paper, looked at it and passed it on. It reached me. I turned it toward the light; apart from a column of numbers, I could see nothing.

So, what was it?

Numbers.

And what conclusion did we draw?

From top to bottom, the numbers increased. It could be a code, or something similar.

Exactly! This was a logbook. A report! First column: dates. Second: pluses and minuses, probably connected with shelling.

Julio took the piece of paper again and involved himself in Dad's agitation. That's right, it could be a report, and the numbers could also be connected with a radio link. Frequencies. Plus, connection established.

Dad stood there, frowning and satisfied: It was he who had found the piece of paper. Luckily! Because it could have been found by someone else . . .

Davor was silent. Granny crunched prestressed cookies from the magic brown bags. I could hear her false teeth clicking. Brkić was collecting stalks of dried coltsfoot on one side of his plate. Mother was gathering crumbs into a little heap in front of her. Sanja was eating as well. She was the only one not to pay any attention to the piece of paper. She ate slowly, chewing lengthily. No doubt she was thinking about the fermenting agents contained in her saliva which assisted digestion. She looked happy, because she was taking vitamins A and C into her organism in a natural form. But Dad, it seemed, was just getting into his stride: What should he, as the person most responsible for the museum, now do? He was holding material evidence that indicated the presence of the fifth column. Should he call the police? Or should we sort it out ourselves? Which one of us wrote this?

The question, however, was not sufficient reason for the picture round the table to change. A five-pointed star of dry coltsfoot stalks, a pyramid of crumbs, a crunching cookie . . .

Finally, Mother looked at the paper: She couldn't see what was so dangerous about that list.

Because it was hidden?

So?

Everything hidden is suspicious. The question arises: Why was it hidden?

Didn't Dad think he was going a bit over the top?

No, he didn't. He was just being cautious. He was not a policeman. He didn't wish to curtail anyone's freedom. If someone thought it was necessary to hide a list of frequencies in the toilet (he looked at Davor), that was his business. But that list . . .

Why was he looking at Davor?

Why shouldn't he look at him?

Fortunately, Julio remembered a story, and there was no fire from this spark. I think that neither Davor nor Dad was sorry. Dad felt that he had been too hasty. Afterward he even confessed that he didn't really mean that business of frequencies, he had just wanted to remind us to be careful, to think about what we said and to whom, and what we left lying about. And Davor didn't feel like yet another quarrel after which he would have to explain yet again to Sanja why he had let himself get involved in it at all. But, this was the third of Julio's stories:

Angtenna
Once I'm on a detail to search apartments. That's back in April. Or is it May? No, April. This apartment's in a building, a council apartment, no, it's May. The second half of May. I remember it was raining. A courier calls me to contact the duty officer. What's up? They're watching television, crack, crackle, they can't hear a thing. What's up? The fifth column has twisted the angtenna. I takes a shooter and goes to the top floor. I knocks on the door, nothing. Tries the handle, locked. I knocks again, the door gives. Whoever's inside keeps quiet. I observes the corridor: There's some saddlebags hanging on the wall. I goes over to search them, only they're not saddlebags, but peasant shoes, hanging from a nail. That tells me I'm dealing with a former peasant. There's a housecoat on a coat hanger, and on its lapel a badge: a crossed hammer and sickle. That tells me his father was a blacksmith and his mother a farmer. I goes into the living room. I sees at once, there's no television, no loudspeaker, or so-called music station. I creeps to the next door. On the way I sees a telephone under an armchair. I connects it, presses the

button to hear who called last, who gave him instructions. Engaged. I hears some wailing. I goes into another room, just as the wall clock in it chimes nine o'clock. I goes closer, and sees not a black cuckoo but a two-headed white eagle, wailing because someone has taken one head off it and painted it black. What can I do, material evidence, I takes down the clock and puts it to one side and carries on. I'll have to look at the terrace, not through the door, but through the bathroom window. On the way I tries the telephone again, still engaged. The bathroom's a veritable treasure trove! A store of military material. Masses of it, half of it not even hidden. I finds: brushes for cleaning cartridge belts, towels for drying off tangks, and detergent for machine washing of caterpillar tires, tampons for gunners, files for making notches in rifle butts, hydrogen for making a hydrogen bomb, lotion for guiding missiles, soap for surprise mine-laying, and all sorts of other things which I packs into a box and puts beside the clock evidence. On the way, I tries the phone again. It rings. Someone responds in Serbo-Montenegrin, the voice is familiar, but I'm hearing it through fog, and then I remembers who it is: my superior commander. I puts the receiver down, then goes back to the bathroom, through the window, onto the terrace. There I finds a mass of tangled and broken wires. Nothing for it, I starts untangling and joining them, until I have just two. As I join them, the scales fall from my eyes: the fifth-column trash has set up a short circuit. I steps back and looks, darkness all around me. I goes back into the room, my material evidence has gone. I race to headquarters, they congratulate me, the angtenna is properly placed now. So why are they sitting in the dark, why aren't they watching the news? There's no power, the fifth column has set up a short circuit somewhere.

In the meantime, Sanja had counted her vitamins and decided to devote a bit of attention to the conversation round the table. She glanced at the list with the numbers on it.

Julio thought it would be best to hand the paper over to the war crimes commission. You never knew with the fifth column.
    Sanja looked at Julio: Did he mean her record?
    What record?

Weight. The first column were dates, the second her weight . . .
And these plus and minus signs?

That's for stools. How regular they are. Plus for when there is one. And minus when there isn't.

There hadn't been one for a whole week!

She'd really prefer not to talk about it at table. Sorry.

Unlike Sanja, Julio would have had seven pluses in one day. We all laughed. And Brkić would have had seven minuses. We all laughed again.

Dad admitted that he was jumpy. He had received an order to evacuate the museum from the building. He would, of course, appeal, but he knew in advance that it wouldn't get him anywhere. This building had once been a school for cadis (judges who judge according to Islamic religious rules) and it seemed that the time had come for it to revert to that. Dad was a historian, so he said all of this calmly. He had learned that the law of the stronger was the foundation of all law. Empires passed across Bosnia like the tides over a sandbank, and judicial decisions and imperial seals lasted as long as words scratched with a finger in the sand. There was no justice nor inequity, no God nor Devil, no victim nor executioner, there were only powerful human passions for correcting old injustices with new ones. It had taken a ruckus to get the museum into this building, it was some kind of justice that it should also be a ruckus that would make it leave, said Dad.

Is that lawful? asked Mother.

Yes. The cadi accuses you, the cadi judges you.

War is not over when the stronger wins, but when the weaker surrenders, said Brkić. Dad looked at him.

A few days went by without my writing anything. Mother was taking longer to sew the balloon because in the meantime she had received an order from commander Junuz to sew several uniforms for his headquarters. He brought black material and a pattern. Something like a car mechanic's overall, only with pockets the shape of crescent rolls. He explained that they were for ammunition. But this is why I hadn't written anything:

Sniffy had begun to be restless, he wanted to go out. He came to me a thousand times, then trotted to the door, and back again. When he started shoving his backside into my lap, thrusting his nose into what I was in the process of writing, I admitted defeat and went with him into the park behind the museum. He made straight for a heap of garbage beside the fence. I repeated eighteen times no and ugh, the jackal kept on rummaging. Davor had told each of us separately, and me in particular, that people put poison that looked like chocolate onto rubbish heaps, and it killed rats quickly and dogs slowly, but both of them without fail.

Then I saw the hyena bringing me something in its jaws, and laying it in front of my feet. It was a human foot. It looked like a joke, like a theatrical prop, like part of a dummy from a shop window, but the fact that I was suddenly bathed in sweat and felt sick told me that it was not black with tar but with dried blood.

I live in the museum like under a glass bell. I write about shells as about theatrical effects, while all around me they dismember people just like me. I don't know what they had done to this foot. I was sick. They poured something over it and set fire to it, then buried it again. Davor rubbed Sniffy's snout with the last dose of Sanja's antiseptic.

Of the several visits to the museum, two were carried out by vets. First a small and elderly one brought, in cooperation with Julio, a cow into our garden. She had eyes like Davor's, large and astounded, and was as thin as him. Although she had milk in her udder, her owner had calculated that he should sell her. There was no food for her, bullets and shells were whistling round her stable, and Julio had also passed by several times.

Whether from sorrow for her calf, or from fear of the shooting and explosions, she had stopped eating. Or perhaps she had eaten all the grass round the headquarters. (Had I already written somewhere that it was virtually a rule that military headquarters should be situated in gardens? The local commanders slept on seven little beds, like Snow White's dwarves.)

The vet examined the cow and said that she had a blockage of the intestines. And that there was no hope for her. Mother took her a bucket of water, stroked the white patch on her forehead, and whispered something to her.

The second vet was a she: Did we have a dog?

Yes.

The veterinary service of the Defense Forces had been charged with making a list of all the dogs with their pedigrees.

I asked why, and I didn't understand the answer. She probably didn't either. That was the only reason why I couldn't say anything more to Davor either. But this was enough: If they came, he wouldn't let them have him.

Who?

Sniffy.

If who came?

The army.

Why should the army come for Sniffy?

To train him.

What for? To bark at shells?

In the Second World War, the Russians had trained Alsatians. They tied explosives to their bodies and sent them under German tanks. That's what they had trained them to do. To crawl under a moving tank. One dog, one tank.

Sniffy was a Dalmatian. A pet. He wasn't a working dog.

He had a pedigree.

But he couldn't be trained. I had spent a whole year teaching him not to jump up at people, so far without any effect. Especially when it was muddy. How many of our neighbors' coats had we washed because of him?

Perhaps they wanted to collect all the dogs so as to send them into the mine-fields round the city?

They didn't need pedigree dogs for that.

Perhaps they were thinking of selling them?

How could someone sell their dog?

Everything was possible . . .

I couldn't bear to go on listening. First I thought that it was because his tearful tone was irritating me. But later I realized that was not the reason. I was frightened, too. After several centuries of war people here are more inclined to believe crazy stories and paranoid predictions than sensible advice and normal expectations.

That same evening in the cellar Julio advised Davor to hide Sniffy.

Why?

Because he, Julio, had heard that they had a plan for these dogs: they'd destroy them and then take photographs. Someone in headquarters had that idea. A good one. In the West people were more inclined to pity pets than people. In Germany, we could ask Granny, there wasn't a wealthy lady who didn't belong to a society for the protection of animals. In capitalism people didn't like each other. The less you liked your neighbor, the more you cared for your dog or cat. Just let ten ladies see Sniffy without legs and ears, and there'd be military intervention.

Julio talked, and Davor watched him. We all knew that this was yet another attack of his imagination, one more story to amuse both us and himself. But a chill spread round our hearts. It would not be the first time someone else's nonsense became our reality overnight.

But he, Julio, would get Sniffy accreditation. He would register him with MUP. (That was the abbreviation used now for the police.) The best way for someone to hide from the army was to be registered with MUP. To be muppified.

Mother started to say something, then bit her tongue. Too late. I had already noticed. She had wanted to ask whether the same thing could be done with her son. She would have liked most of all to shepherd him to crouch under her skirt. And she would have been as happy as a hen on an egg.

A wooden egg.

Mrs. Flintstone arrived on the wings of rosy-fingered dawn. She had brought Sanja two eggs for frying and a piece of real live cheese, with real live holes in it. She was all fired up, she had gone the day before to get another lunch packet, a French one, in a box, this big. Inside were fire lighters (in fact, little rolls, that you lit and burned, to heat cans from the aforementioned packet), but our little one had thought they were sweets and ate them.

Mother assured her it would all be all right. The child was quite cheerful this morning, he had been playing, he didn't have a temperature, Fata shouldn't worry.

Fata had heard that Mother knew about dousing and plumb lines?

Mother, of course, corrected her: Plumb lines, acupuncture, *I Ching,* macrobiotics. She didn't know anything about dousing.

Fine! And could Mother come and check whether their beds were turned the right way?

Mother hadn't done that for a long time.

It wouldn't have to take her long now either.

And why was it so important for Fata?

She kept having dreams. She really had a hard time in her sleep. A whole chicken of weight fell off her during the night. And she had acquired schizophrenia of the neck.

All right, what was so terrible about dreaming?

She dreamed last night that she was being chased by a shell. And the shell had wings, and kept running after her, crowing. And it had a head like her Junuz. That must be because of the bed. Before, she used to forget what she dreamed. But now even when she was awake she thought here comes Junuz about to attack her.

Mother then excused herself. She had begun the lunch, she was sewing uniforms, there wasn't a plumb line, they'd left it behind in Dobrinje . . .

And she couldn't do it without a plumb line?

No.

Julio could, however. He materialized from somewhere and offered to do it himself, with a divining rod.

When would that be?

In the afternoon. After he'd cut a good rod.

They'd expect him.

No need. What was important was the radiation. Bioenergy. Waves. If she came this afternoon with coffee, he'd have everything ready.

That afternoon, while we were drinking and smelling the beverage called life, Julio established a diagnosis. Mrs. Flintstone did not understand the greater part of it, but the story was certainly not intended for her. Julio was amusing himself at Mother's expense:

Fata's mantra was giving off good vibrations, there were biomagnetic forces in the field. The chakra of her appendix was no good. Because of Ping. Ping and Li Ping, the point of transcendental integration. Bramasutra had summoned karmasutra, and her sex chakra was out of balance.

Mrs. Flintstone asked whether they could manage without sex.

No. The bed chakra could not be considered without the sex chakra. That's why it would be good for her to eat pies made of late spinach, and walnuts with honey.

Mother smiled, but she wasn't pleased. She sensed a joke at her expense, this was nothing new, either in style or wit. Mother was cross that Fata, who was genuinely interested in plumb lines and divining, had got involved in her battle with Brkić. (And Mother was driven in her battle with Brkić, or rather, for Brkić, by that exalted patience and belief in success, that only rare missionaries have. Brkić was everything she was not: an unbeliever and a communist, a carnivore and drunkard, irascible and stubborn, a Don Quixote who knew he was attacking windmills. In that battle Julio was Rosinante, but neither Brkić nor Mother told him that.)

■ □ ■ □ ■

CHAPTER SEVEN

The story of the Gordian cow. Archimedes' barrel. Man's best friend.
Life returns to the old graves. Black butterflies and yellow flowers.
The Tunnyel. A fruit tree by the highway.

AFTER A LONG TIME, WE SMELLED AGAIN THE AROMA OF GREASY
roast meat, which made Granny more edgy than all the shellings up
to now put together. Even Brkić had put on his better trousers. Julio
had brought Mother, instead of a bouquet of flowers, a bouquet of
lettuce wrapped in newspaper.

Sanja, Davor, and I were not looking forward to lunch. We knew
where it came from. In the smoke that rose from the barbecue, I
saw the cow and her large sad eyes. When the vet had announced
his sentence, blockage of the intestines, the logisticians reacted in a
flash: the sooner she was slaughtered, the less time she would have
to get thin, and the less thin she was, the more meat could be got
from her. It turned out, however, that it was more difficult to
slaughter a cow than, say, a Chetnik.

First they approached her with a knife from behind. She had a pre-
monition of evil and resisted. She kicked and mooed, fought,
and finally the commander cut the Gordian cow. He drew out his pistol and fired it at the white patch between the cow's eyes. One bullet
was not enough. The cow just spread her front legs and was quiet for
a moment and then began to twist and moo still more loudly.

The commander emptied his whole charger. The cow knelt. She
fell silent. All that could be heard was her loud breathing. She
looked at the commander with her enormous eyes. From time to
time somewhere under her skin a muscle would twitch then stop.

Then, straight from the film *Terminator* the commander was brought a rifle known as "the pump." That rifle bore the cow away to the eternal shores of the Ganges. The vet examined the body, admitted that her intestines were not blocked, but such mistakes were not rare. It was harder to be a vet than a doctor, because animals couldn't say what hurt them. Then he set about removing cutlets and steaks.

A table was laid in the garden, the stove brought out, fire set, the barbecue lit. A harmonica was played, there was shooting into the air, singing (How strong the gadfly must be, to drive the spotted cow from under her tree, Ho!), shrieking, and cursing. Then the cow's head was brought before the commander. Shiny with melted butter, the glassy eyes gazed at him. And he turned the head, together with the dish, first in one direction, then the other, stood up theatrically, aimed and delivered a karate chop to the nape. Both glassy balls flew out of the buttered hollows and rolled over the table. In my homeland, this blow is valued like a degree from Yale in America or a goal in the final of the World Cup in Brazil.

As the reader who is a good judge of human character has already guessed, my brother, Davor, decided to ignore the existence of military service and constant requests to respond to the call for general mobilization. Davor behaved toward the fighters who passed through our street and the museum, like Archimedes toward the Roman soldiers: Don't touch my circles.

He would certainly be quite safe in the museum, no one would touch him, check his credentials, investigate his case. At least for a certain time. But, because of our inquisitive and envious neighbors, it became necessary to maintain the illusion that he was still working at the Radio. Every morning, about nine o'clock, he went to work. He usually put on a red jacket, blue trousers and white gym shoes, because they were the colors of the Serbian flag, at which snipers wouldn't shoot. However, yesterday morning he put on new jeans, a shirt, jacket, even shoes put by for after the war. Sanja stopped making a snowman out of Sniffy's shed hairs: Why was he dressed like that?

Because it was a nice day. Because he felt good. Because he might even call in at the Radio. Why did she ask?

Because it wasn't easy to wash and iron all that. Or maybe he thought that washing and ironing did themselves? When was he coming back? (Sometime.) Where was he going? (Here and there.) He should take care. They'd said there'd be shelling today.

They say that every day.

Did he have to go today? Couldn't he go tomorrow instead . . .

They'd say there'd be shelling tomorrow as well.

But tomorrow maybe Sanja wouldn't have a bad dream. She had a principle she adhered to. Although her dreams intimated and foresaw if not events then at least lucky and unlucky days, she never tried to convince others of their message. She bore the burden of her dreams herself.

Davor finally left the museum, officially for the Radio, but unofficially to mooch around town, collect material for some future radio play, and buy cheap books. (Only books could be bought with coupons. Now and then there would be a misunderstanding about the number of noughts rubbed out of the prewar prices, but such differences were negligible. Books were even sold out of abandoned apartments, books that the new tenants exchanged for cigarettes. Books with the owner's signature on the first page.) According to the old rule that it was easiest to hide in a crowd, Davor spent most of his time in the market.

Of course, the police knew that rule as well. Men would be taken off to obligatory work. Obligatory work consisted, for the most part, of digging trenches. Trenches were dug on the front lines, toward the Serbian positions. Fortunately, Davor was in luck. He was given the task of extracting oil from the boiler house in a cellar.

Oil is, as everyone knows, propulsion fuel for cars of the Golf Diesel make. At first it was taken from abandoned gas pumps. Then out of private cars, then out of state bulldozers, buses, cranes. And finally out of boiler-houses and power plants.

While Davor and the other detainees carried canisters out of the cellar and climbed with them onto the truck, passing among the barrels and pouring oil into them, the sheikh's people heckled them, waved their automatic rifles around, and forced them to work faster. One came right up to Davor's face, and together with a voice from his transistor he sang a song about himself. About heroes and defenders of the city, the same song about whose author Davor had not wanted to make a program, and because of which he had been directed to "rest." Bloodshot eyes, a sparse beard, and just as brown and sparse teeth.

When he got home and approached Sanja, presumably to tell her all about it, she passed by him as past a garbage dump. He didn't cry at the time probably only because dumps don't cry. I didn't hear them speak at all that day. I don't know who was the first to break the silence and choose peace rather than war, music rather than silence, life rather than death (I listened to the radio today!), but I had the opportunity to record the following:

In the truck, three full barrels, four empty, one on-going. An Ustasha with an automatic guarding the door. Davor was taking care not to get his new jeans greasy and trying to make sure that the Ustashas didn't notice, because they would have dirtied them on purpose.

Had she known, she would have received him differently.

How could she know, if she didn't ask and didn't listen.

Why didn't he put himself in her position. She had no one apart from him. It was normal for her to be worried. She would like it if some time it could be her who went out and him who had to wait. Telling him she would be back at twelve, and coming at three.

Davor raised his eyes. Sanja apologized: She was tired, on edge, she hadn't meant that.

Didn't she feel well?

Problems with her stools again. She hadn't been to the toilet for several days.

Did she want some tea? (In a jar that had the status of a funeral urn, we kept the dust of one of the knights of the order of the emptied gut. I know, I'm being sarcastic. I can't reconcile myself to the fact that love, and the two of them love each other, permits one to talk in its garden with so much sorrow and joy about something that concerns the large intestine!)

No, thanks. She'd try again today.

What had she eaten?

It wasn't the food. (It's hard to help some people, because their problem is never where it could be resolved.)

So what was it?

She was afraid of rats. (He held her hand, she her stomach. He put his arm round her shoulder, she nestled her head into its resting place. That's the bit on my brother, between his chin, shoulders, and chest.) She had heard that now, when there was no water, rats were having orgies in the sewers, looking for food, and they even came up through the pipes and out into toilet bowls. Even when there were people on them.

Rats! Ugh! That'll teach me to eavesdrop. I'm more afraid of those creatures than anything else. Even more than mice. Of course I'm not including earwigs, I don't know how afraid of them I am, because I faint as soon as I see them. (Mrs. Flintstone: When you see an earwig, get off your horse and squash it with your foot!) I entirely understand Sanja's justified closure. Now what happened to Davor doesn't seem that terrible after all.

It's time for me to acquaint the patient reader with some of my reflections on literature, for which I should owe most thanks to my teacher.

The question of the narrator in a work of prose: As everyone knows, the narrator is not a specific character, but a function. If we compare it with film, he is not the cameraman, but the camera. The narrator is the medium through which a connection is established between the writer and his characters, and also between those characters and the reader.

In concrete terms, in practice, in my case, it isn't that simple. Because the people around me are not characters. They are my family. The events are not arranged into a plot. They constitute my life. Consequently, I can't be a function either. For, if I am a camera, who is then holding the camera? God? A Muse? Immeasurable talent? (Here I got to thinking a bit. And reached one temporarily satisfactory answer: I am a divided being. One Maja writes, draws conclusions, makes judgments, chats with her future reader, while the other, her servant, slave, hired gun, does her dirty work for her: peers through keyholes, rubs her cheek against slightly open doors, sunbathes in the shade under broken doors, sets up mirrors like horizontal periscopes. She even sometimes reads other people's papers, thumbs through other people's books, sticks her nose into other people's rooms and belongings.)

Every day that passes is one day of war less. That's what the optimists think. Every day that passes is one day of war more, that's what the pessimists say. Our shifts in the porter's lodge have fallen into a rhythm. Brkić and I like the dawn. He thinks about his barge on the Sava, or his village on two rivers, from where he once set out into the world, while I have peace and light for writing.

Mother likes the shift up to midnight. Julio the one after that. It's when you sleep best. Dad and Davor replace one another in an orderly way. My duty in the morning shift is to prepare fuel for the fire and water for the drinks that from inertia we call coffee, but all it has in common with coffee is the pot it's made in. Those drinks, so-called coffee surrogates, are chicory, dandelion, Russian tea, Earl Grey, English breakfast, cocoa, roast lentil, rice, bran, and all possible combinations of the above.

After I have removed the blackout from the windows and let light into our fortress, sometimes I listen to the muffled conversation in my brother's sleeping-chamber. After such wakings, he is gloomy all day. As though someone had emptied a dustbin over his head. At such times, all that Davor, whom no one liked or understood, had was Sniffy, and the two of them had a training lesson.

Some day I'll demonstrate that the character of a dog doesn't differ in any way from the character of a person. Every person is a servant, ready to beg or jump up, fetch, offer his paw, roll onto his back. Even when he refuses to do these things, it's not because of pride, but because of the inadequate reward. Sniffy is a grudge-bearer who doesn't have the courage to bite. When he barks, he does it to protect himself, not us. When he crawls into our beds, under our blankets, it's not in order to warm up our feet, but so that we can warm his back. When he licks our hand, it's not a sign of love, he's collecting the scents of food from our skin. He doesn't look one in the eye, but the mouth.

Am I describing Sniffy or Davor?

Davor has taught Sniffy to bark when someone knocks at the door. When Sanja, informing us of her latest health bulletin, knocked three times on wood, Sniffy got up and went to bark at the front door. Then Davor got up and went to open the door. He remained convinced that it was Fata's children having a game.

The act of training itself is a successful substitute for watching television. For instance, Davor gives Sniffy the command to sit, Sniffy lies down. Davor tells him to stand in the showing pose, Sniffy sits down and waits for a reward. Davor tells him to fetch his ball, he comes back with a rubber Miss Piggy. Then he rolls onto his back, raises all four legs in the air and waits for a reward again. He looks at the piece of dry bread in Davor's hand. All the dogs I know have such an expression, perfidious, greedy, and infinitely sad, all at the same time.

Granny died. She was buried in the Lav cemetery. That's an old cemetery that came to life again in the war. Life returns to old graveyards.

I wasn't allowed to attend the funeral. The cemetery is in bullet's reach of the Serbosnipers. A few days ago they had targeted a funeral. People were injured. Davor, who knows how and what I'm writing, ceded me one detail: The years of birth and death on the grave markers, and the letters of the names of the buried, are molded of plastic and nailed to the piece of wood. There are so many dead that the figure 9 has been used up, and instead they are now using the letter P back to front.

Granny was buried quickly. Like going through the checkout at a department store. Brkić didn't go. He stayed to look after the museum. In fact, he stayed to get drunk.

So, Granny died.

She died suddenly, like everyone who has been dying for a long time. I catch myself putting crusts of warm bread aside for her. My Mother is no longer anyone's child now. When she had had a good cry and slept, she woke up older. She looked like Granny. Only now did I see how gray her hair had gone in the last few months.

It was Brkić who found Granny, on his morning shift. He had not wanted to wake us. That she was no more, we each learned individually. When I saw her dead for the first and last time, she was lying in her little room, with a bouquet of roses above her head, painted onto the white metal headboard.

She died in the rocking chair. With her little suitcase on her knee. A bit from Brkić, a bit from Davor, but most from Julio, I learned the following: The night before, in one of those shellings when the sound of the explosions reminds one of children running over the tin roof of a garage or a wooden stick being dragged across the lace of iron railings, the Vijećnica caught fire. This was the building where the National and University Library was situated. Many books were burned. Brkić brought Granny several silver-black butterflies with patterns on them in the shape of letters.

Granny was pleased with this unusual gift. The whole morning, while gunshots cracked in the hills like woodpeckers, she sat in her rocking chair. In front of her, on two little tables made of piled-up paintings, various little bottles were arranged. I used to think they were perfumes, a memento from part of Granny's life. Later I saw that that wasn't it. Granny kept all kinds of things in those little bottles, without rhyme or reason, powders and fluids, herbs and spices, and other things I never quite worked out.

When I went in to call her for coffee (and to see what she was up to!), she was holding her suitcase and on it was a book snatched from the ash. She was crumbling the burned pages in her fingers, and kneading it with some other potion in her hand. And sniffing it.

Mother told me: In the last war, Granny had had a relationship with a German officer. The end of the war had put a stop to it. Granny stayed in Belgrade, with her sick stepfather. People turned their heads away from her. When, despite them, she didn't bow hers, they began to say that the whore should be arrested and shaved. Her stepfather, a history teacher, did all he could to send Granny out of the country. That was neither possible nor did she want to leave him as he was ill. It was winter. There was no wood, and what could be bought at a high price, no one wanted to sell to them. They burned old clothes, furniture, and finally, books. Then, they got subtenants. Two young Partizans, officers. Although they knew everything about her, they both fell in love with her. Her stepfather died. They helped her leave the country.

After the night when the Vijećnica burned down, the morning broke yellow and warm. In clouds of smoke, whirlpools of scorched pages flew, like flocks of sparrows.

For my European readers here are three fundamental facts about the building called the Vijećnica: 1. Crown Prince Franz Ferdinand emerged from it as he hurried to his meeting with Gavrilo Princip; 2. It was where the biggest and best-equipped library in the city and whole republic was situated; 3. It was built in a pseudo-Moorish style, that is a mixture of Austrian and Arab architecture, with a colored façade that peeled of its own accord every third year, like me when I get burned sunbathing.

Everyone was desolate and embittered because of the burned building and destroyed books. Most of all those who had never been in it and who had never read anything other than the newspaper in which their vegetables were wrapped at the market. Dad, the exception that proves the above rule, was beside himself. In the whole of history the only thing similar to this vandalism he could think of was the Barbarian attack on Rome.

Davor could not avoid asking whether in this case the Serbs were the Barbarians. Dad said yes. Then Davor asked who were the Romans.

Sanja got involved. And Mother thought that was enough. And Julio had a coughing fit. As for me, I agreed. I really wouldn't like this to be one of the themes of my novel. But it looks as though it can't be avoided. I'm making such an effort not to mention the names of the peoples and nations in these territories, because they stink on the page like a rotten tooth in the mouth. As though in the street where the narrator is walking manholes had been opened up and the foul steam and stench of the sewers gushed out of them.

When these things are discussed, faces harden, lips stretch, sweat breaks out on foreheads, necks, and under noses. People wave their arms, shout, threaten, and swear. That is the way conversations about nations end up. And I mention this because of my sense that the roots of this yellow stinking flower above the Vijećnica are using their tentacles and fibers to suck the blood from Dad and Davor's veins.

Then, by way of a conclusion, Davor said roughly this: Before the war, the Serbs lived in one state. With other peoples. But those peoples said that they were under threat in that state, because the Serbs had privileges. And each of them wanted their own state. The Serbs raised the question of borders. Here are states for you all, but we are not giving up our land. The Muslims then said that without that land their state was small. There were more Serbs, they had an army, weapons, personnel. And the Muslims wailed like a spoiled brat who wanted to grab the swing from a stronger child and was shouting for its mummy to help. And its mummy was Europe, the world, America, the Islamic Conference.

The Serbs destroyed, burned, looted, raped. They said they were defending their own land, while they were plundering other people's. They were protecting their own people, and persecuting the others.

That was all being done by individuals. And there were individuals like that among the Muslims as well. Everyone raped and looted and destroyed and burned. Wherever they could and as it suited them!

Dad thought Davor was a Chetnik. Only he was too much of a coward to go and join them and do all the things that he was justifying.

First, he was not justifying it, he condemned it. He condemned the act. And justice would catch up with the guilty, when the war was over. Second, in this city whoever is not prepared to spit on the Serbs is a Chetnik. He, Davor, was not going to spit on anybody!

Wasn't he ashamed of talking like that? Wasn't he ashamed in the face of all these graves? All these maimed people? Murdered children?

Why? Because he had been more fortunate up to now?

Why hadn't he prevented it!

How?

By not hiding behind a pregnant woman's skirts. He could have taken a rifle.

And then what? Kill his relatives on the other side? Become a holy martyr?

What's wrong with that?

Everyone knows who the martyrs are. What they're fighting and dying for.

The martyrs are part of a culture and a tradition. Which he does not accept. Only he doesn't have the guts to say so. Because if he did, he'd be asked why he wasn't up there, on the hill.

Luckily for all of us, we heard the clumping of Mrs. Flintstone's wooden-soled shoes. She had come to offer Mother her condolences. Let Mother not grieve, Allah took only the best to Himself, and not everyone is destined to be a holy martyr. Fata is full of optimism. Her Junuz says that the Serbomontenegrin aggressor is winding down, that they had the umbrella. (That's what people call the campaign of prohibiting flights over the territory of our country.) Meanwhile, ours were digging a tunnel, only it was a secret. A tunnel under the ground. Our fighters and defenders would then use that tunnel to get out of the city and attack the enemy from behind.

Mother smiled and thanked her very much, both for this comfort and for the bag Mrs. Flintstone had brought, and which Julio had already taken and removed from it a jar of coffee and a box of sugar cubes. He confirmed that the story of the tunnel was not an invention. He was one of the first to have applied here the Vietcong tactic of tunnel warfare.

The Tunnyel
My superior command asks me are there any volunteers. What for? To liquidate the nest. It isn't letting us open our eyes. Why didn't we send in a grenade? We did, but it fell on us instead. Luckily it was locally produced, so it didn't explode. In that case, I'm ready. I takes another couple of lads with me, and for weapons we takes a spade for me and buckets for them, for removing the earth, and we sets off to dig a tunnyel in order to sneak up on the nest from behind. After about fifty yards, my spade hits a cable. I sees that it's a telephone line, so I have a listen. Some warlord is calling his wife: she shouldn't expect him for dinner. She's cross, she's made stewed sauerkraut, and he explains that the enemy has prepared a diversion. Well, great, not to disappoint him, I goes on. Then my spade hits a wall. Right, left, up, down, until I find a window and enter the dugout. Before the ethnic cleansing, Illyrians used to live here. I find two little coffee cups from the lower stone age and a coffee pot from the upper copper age. Then, someone knocks on the door. I

goes to dig it out, and standing there is comrade Tito. I stands to attention, banging my head on the *stećak*, what are you doing here, comrade? What can you do! The Banović miners have marched on Parliament. They tells me to go further in, it's swarming with Chetniks up there, they keep getting so far and someone collapses into their tunnyel. I goes on, catches on a wire again. I listens. Never mind that she's made the sauerkraut, she could invite some lieutenant to dinner. Her husband won't be there, they're expecting a diversion. In that case, here's the lieutenant. Just then I sees that I've crossed into Serbian territory. Every so often there'd be some bones, then a thatched hut, then a piece of canvas, and in the canvas a machine gun and a picture of King Peter, and to one side piles of paper. By the stench I see that the Belgrade newspaper *Politika* and weekly *Nin* have been cut up and scrumpled. Then I make my way up and come out just where I thought: behind that nest. And in it something, either a woman, or a clean-shaven Chetnik. Polished nails, but hairy hands. It has a mustache, and listick. On its cap is a five-pointed star, but round its neck a crucifix. And as it fires a bullet, it gives the rifle butt a slap with that cross. I raises my spade, but all at once a hole opens up in the earth and the creature falls into it. I peers over the edge, and from the hole I hear miners singing: In the tunnyel in the dark, the fleur-de-lis emits a spark.

Several days passed since Granny's departure for the fields of eternal lavender. In my Diary she twinkled like a shooting star passing over the end of the sky. Davor was considering shooting a play about her. About her life. I asked him who would be interested in such a thing.

Every item finds a buyer, and every play an audience. He would introduce a bit of intrigue. Maybe Granny had not died of another stroke.

What did he mean?

The room was dark. The holes in the window and door frames had been filled in. It was all crammed with exhibits, stifling with dust. Maybe she suffocated. When Brkić had found her in the morning, all the little bottles in front of her were open and empty. Maybe her perfumes and scents suffocated her.

It didn't seem likely. She was lying back in the rocking chair, as though she were sleeping.

Why had she kept those little bottles? Why had she opened them? To remember the past.

That's right. She had mixed up all the scents. That was in Proust. His great novel was conceived in the smell of a little cake. It seems that smells have access to those shelves of the brain where sight, hearing, and touch cannot reach. But why had she opened all those bottles?

Yes, why?

Perhaps she wanted to learn something. To see her whole life, at a glance. Or to peer into what was in store for her.

Davor was right, that could make an interesting play. But Davor didn't go out anywhere, he had time to occupy himself with such things. Sanja was well, and I was allowed to take Sniffy out. In the streets the campaign Digging for Victory was in train, it reminded one a bit of films about the Germans and the Jews.

Everyone whom Sniffy takes for a walk has a longer left arm than right, a dislocated shoulder, and dry lips from the constant repetition of no, ugh, leave it, heel, don't pull. We take him out to do his business, which he does without fail in front of at least a dozen observers. His favorite surfaces are cobbles, steps in front of other people's doors, flower beds, and the top of someone's pile of fine sand. I would most like to pretend that I don't know him, but, partly because I'm at the other end of the leash, but also because of Davor's insistence on a report on the state and quality of the stool, which is the best indicator of canine health and mood, that is not possible.

Walking with him is a sport, a mixture of waterskiing, throwing the hammer, a trotting race, and pole vaulting. The pole is the piece of wood I throw for him to bring back, and which in the end I go to fetch, while he shoves his snout into a can or jumps with muddy paws all over ladies in light-colored skirts. All of this, however, is bearable in comparison with the twenty-eight minutes I spent waiting for him to have intimate relations with a Bosnian Yarddog bitch. Must I emphasize that he hit the jackpot in front of several dozen observers, whose congratulations and praise were conveyed to me, rather than to him.

On my way back from the walk, I came upon Mrs. Flintstone who had just come upon Mother with her question: What was Davor's status? She hadn't seen him going to work in the morning for several days now. Did the doggy know where his master was? Godsave his spots!

Mother's answer, that Davor was on leave, merely provoked curiosity: That was the first time Mrs. Flintstone had heard such a thing. Perhaps Davor had lied. Perhaps he had been fired. As far as she was aware, since the beginning of the aggression against sovereign BH, no one had been given any leave. Her Junuz had been in the war-torn peripheral areas of the city since the very first day. (Was this going to become a general phenomenon, that people start speaking in phrases they hear a dozen times a day from their transistors? Brkić: Power stinks from the tongue down.)

Of course, someone who talks like Mrs. Flintstone seeks an appropriate collocutor: What did the Doctor think, would there be foreign intervention?

The Doctor didn't believe in such a thing.

Nor did Mrs. Flintstone. Uprofop was a crook. (Uprofop was a word from the language which some now call their mother tongue, and others Bosnian. It grew out of the English abbreviation UNPROFOR, which was used to indicate soldiers in blue helmets and white vehicles, so-called transporters. If this war could be imagined as a competition, Uprofop would be the referee. And in the local terrain, as long as the visitors were winning, the referee could only be a crook.) Mrs. Flintstone had heard that they went to Pale every day to share a spit-roast lamb with the Aggressor. That was why Uprofop was a Chetnik, too!

Julio, on the other hand, thought that there would be American intervention. They had to try out their new weapons. They had some rays, and when they were aimed at asphalt, it melted and became like dough. All the Serbian runways would melt. They had some other rays, they turned oil to vinegar. They could curdle things, with their tanks.

The Americans were the only decent people. A great nation.

That was science. The military industry. Now they had some kind of positron bomb. It was even better than the neutron bomb. It didn't affect civilians, but snuffed whoever was a soldier.

How could it tell the difference between a soldier and a civilian?

The CIA had mobilization lists.

The bomb, how did the bomb tell the difference?

Ah, the bomb. It had a computer inside it, and photographs. They had photographed everyone. From up there. From a satellite. Now, whenever they felt like it, they could hear what we were saying down here. That was power.

And what did the bomb do when it exploded?

It didn't explode. It flew in a circle, casually. And when it saw an aggressor, bash. It had a pneumatic paddle. Like a fly swatter, only bigger. It splattered a person before he could say knife. He didn't need a car or a stretcher. That was why the Russians were interested in disarmament.

Julio never told lies, which was why he was often obliged to invent the truth. Anyone who didn't know him would have said he was a clown. And they would be wrong. Behind their cheerful make-up, clowns conceal weary hearts and sorrowful thoughts. Julio had no make-up and he concealed nothing. I'm beginning to see why Mother once said of him that in his next life he would be a drinking fountain by the roadside.

This is how Julio sent me for kebabs (tricked me, fooled me, wittily and astutely joked at my expense). He asked Dad whether he could take the big national cookery book from the library and sell it. Dad didn't know that there was such a book, but anyway he couldn't. I'm surprised that I didn't suspect something the minute he asked Dad such a thing. When he moves carbon paper from one drawer to another, Dad makes out a receipt for himself and signs it.

I don't think that I've written anything yet about my wartime hobby: browsing through cookery books. Cheese, eggs, pickled cucumber, stuffed peppers, hot pretzels, butter, white coffee, hot dogs, mustard, meat pie, yogurt, moussaka, ajvar, marzipan, French fries . . . There, my saliva is dripping onto the paper. But I'll say it's tears.

So, I went into the library to see that cookery book of Julio's and nearly bumped into his apprentice. Who still looks like Tom Cruise. What could I do, I said hi. And he said hi. He was holding onto an encyclopedia, while I had hold of the door handle: Could I help him with anything?

He had come to find and look through some books with photographs of *stećaks*. A friend had asked him. No one had yet thought of making earrings like little Bosnian shields. Or images from the *stećaks*. His friend was a goldsmith. They had made this earring together.

He turned his ear to me, and I had to admit, to myself of course, that I would have been glad to wear one like that. It was made of gold, and shaped like a miniature and faithful replica of an old Bosnian shield. I sought a good shield to shield me, then I threw the good shield away, for it weighs on me. Mak Dizdar.

It got on my nerves that he was fiddling about among the books, and so I offered to find and copy appropriate illustrations and motifs for him. By tomorrow. When I was left alone, I took a fat book with pictures and drawings in color, and that book was not a cookery book. And it was not the only one of that kind which I leafed through that afternoon. Now I'm quite bewildered by what I've discovered: Bosnia is for him his homeland. It is an old country, it had kings with golden crowns, crowns with the fleur-de-lis, knights with sabers, fortresses with gates and towers. Bosnia is a small country, you can put it in your pocket. People there live with open palms. Bosnia is a country from which there is no place to run, except among the stars. It is a shepherd's summer shelter made of rock in the karst. Bosnia is a fruit tree beside the highway, which sets fruit every year, but it never manages to ripen. (I'll have to stop. If I go on like this, I'll be made a member of the Writers' Union.)

■ □ ■ □ ■

CHAPTER EIGHT

Delirium gravidae. The European garbage dump. The walking Ooof.
The nightmare of Cleopatra's cats. The noose round Davor tightens.

ON THE NEWS THIS MORNING, BABIES HAD DIED. THERE WAS NO OIL
for the generators, and they had to turn off the incubators at the
maternity hospital. Sanja sat on the edge of her bed, with her hands
together thrust between her knees. She rocked backwards and for-
wards, chewed her lower lip and stared through the wall straight at
the switched-off glass boxes. What if her baby arrived early?

Impossible! She had a cervical cerclage.

What did Davor know? It was impossible for there not to be oil
for the incubators, but there wasn't.

There was a war on.

Even if there was a war on, her baby could still come early. If she
could only fall asleep and never wake up again. Just not to be.

She shouldn't say such things.

She said what she was thinking.

Then she shouldn't think such things.

She was sick of it all. Fear, and anxiety, and insomnia, and moni-
toring, did she have a temperature, was she bleeding, was the baby
moving . . .

Why shouldn't it move?

Because she was completely terrified. Tense, constantly tense.
Rigid. She slept badly, she ate badly. It wasn't good for the baby in
her stomach.

That wasn't true! Her baby was taking all it needed from her.

But she didn't have all the baby needed.

Yes, she did.

Oh God, he talked as though she were an idiot. As though she enjoyed being afraid. She didn't know what to do with herself she was so bored! And she had imagined those poor babies. In reality everything was sweetness and light.

No, but it wasn't all so black, either.

She still wanted to die.

She shouldn't talk like that.

Yes, she should. As far as he was concerned, she was nothing but a source of food for his baby. Hummus!

It was their baby.

She didn't need it!

Crying, sobbing, whimpering, whispering. Probably pills, Valium, so-called happy pills. Then she slept, while he walked around with swollen lids and bloodshot eyes. In the afternoon, again: Nothing smells like a pregnant woman.

She didn't smell.

That's right! She stank. It wasn't surprising that Granny had died.

She was exaggerating.

OK, she was exaggerating. Look! There were even flies on her!

And she stood up abruptly and gave herself a slap. The fly fled. She picked up a baby's onesie and lashed into the insect world. How did she come by a onesie? Ah, that was an object with a special reference. Mrs. Flintstone had brought it. She and Sanja were very much in love. I think I understand why. Mrs. Flintstone is impressed by Sanja's kindness, education, upbringing. While Sanja at last has someone who will listen to her attentively. Their conversation goes roughly like this:

Sanja's intestinal peristalis was upset. Her digestive tract wasn't functioning properly.

Did she have a blockage or henterocolitis?

A blockage. On a psychological basis.

Was she taking anything for her nerves?

Sometimes. She had a uterus bicornis, with suspected uterus du-plex. That's why they'd done the cerclage. She fell pregnant easily, but it was hard for her to carry to term. It all depended where the gestational sac had lodged.

When Mrs. Flintstone had her first baby, her Roki weighed only six kilos. The doctor told her to buy him a school bag at once. And she hadn't even known she was pregnant until the fifth month.

Wasn't she nauseous?

Yes, but she thought it was a hangover. Had she heard this one: A peasant has three pleasures: eating, drinking, and throwing up! Had her breasts swollen?

A bit.

Mrs. Flintstone had worn a 40 as a girl. And while she was preg-nant, a 42. Did Sanja want a cigarette?

Half.

Take a whole one. Her Junuz had brought them today. Drina with a filter. As long as they weren't Morava. Drina was like Marl-boro compared to Morava.

I have to confess that I missed the moment when Julio brought in a heap of lunch packets. It was only this morning, when I was coming back from jogging with Sniffy, that I saw him throwing the boxes out of the cellar window.

He was throwing out boxes and throwing in canisters. Of oil. Which was not for incubators. (In the meantime I had heard that the business with the incubators was a hoax. Each incubator had its own generator, and they didn't need much oil. So who spreads such morbid news among the people? They falsify the numbers of the dead, raped, and hounded out. Why?)

Julio had done good business. He had given the lunch packets to the local commander (that's what Unprofor called Junuz and other similar leaders of the resistance movement) and got oil in exchange. Where from? From boiler-houses (Davor knew more about that) and from power plants. When eventually, in a decade or two, some-one repairs the pipeline, there still won't be any power, because the power plants won't be able to function.

Davor was furious because of the black market. Although neither he nor Dad finds a cause for a quarrel essential, this one is always within reach and welcome.

According to Davor, sufficient food is arriving in the city. But the Muslim government has organized the distribution so that the citizens, to whom the food belongs, come last. It's distributed first to the army, the police, charitable organizations, soup kitchens, and who knows to what other priorities. In all the headquarters, they stuff themselves with cucumber, paprika, meat, cheeses, wine, and whisky. And the citizens, humiliated and scared to death, can only watch while the heaps of garbage outside those headquarters grow. We've got what the government promised. Europe has finally reached us. So far only in the form of other people's garbage dumps, but the process is underway.

Dad couldn't see why Davor thought that the city authorities were Muslim. The Presidency included both Serbs and Croats.

Yes. But the Serbs in that Presidency were like eunuchs. In serious matters, no one took them seriously.

No! I'm not going on about the two of them again. I do it subconsciously. Everyone talks the way Dad and Davor do. So, I think, it'll be interesting for the reader. But it isn't for me. I wanted to make a note of Julio's transaction.

Namely, a little later, he exchanged the oil for boxes of ammunition. He sold the ammunition (Two bullets for one German mark. Cheap!) and bought two full gas cylinders. The cylinders were handed over to Brkić. The balloon-filling was set for roughly a week's time.

Today I learned that laying hens were now so hungry that they were eating the eggs they had just laid. Today I found Dad quarreling with the radio. Today I learned that Julio calls Sanja the walking Ooof. Today the kids promoted Sniffy to founder of a new breed: the American piebald. They tumbled into the museum and asked: How's Sniffy? They had heard from Davor that we had bathed him, and that all his spots had come off.

They were all terribly worried, even unhappy I'd say.

———————

Really, why is he so popular? How is it that he manages so easily, without the least effort, to captivate everyone he lollops past, his ears flapping like wings? This is what I think: His whiteness makes him clean and shiny, and that's a quality that wins over women like Mrs. Flintstone. He is emphatically freckled, with black rings round his eyes, and almost completely black ears, which is also very much prized by connoisseurs of dogs. He is a rare and expensive breed, and is, therefore, congenial to snobs. He is cheerful and harmless, and that appeals to children and young parents.

But the reason why he appeals to everyone, without distinction or exception, is the fact that, the way he is, despite everything, he has stayed with us, he has not been abducted, abandoned, or betrayed like so many other pedigree dogs. He is the embodiment of what Sarajevo once was and what, despite everyone and everything, it is trying to remain.

His ancestors were the nightmare which meant that Cleopatra's cats never managed to get any shut-eye. They hunted with Dalmatian nobles, accompanied English ladies, and enchanted Disney. That is what people feel here, although they don't know it, and that is why, when they smile at him, it's as though they were mocking those who are destroying the city and killing people.

Mother and I were in the atrium, drinking a mixture of roasted bran and barley. The satellite, which was photographing us sitting out in the open, drinking brown gold, knew that yesterday evening the Barbarians did not catapult the city. We slept calmly and dreamed images of peacetime.

Mother drank her coffee quickly, hurrying to send Saibaba asanas and lotus flowers. Dad had shaved with his least blunt razor, after he had lathered himself with a paint-brush. Brkić was cutting out joining pieces for the balloon gas cylinder, Sanja and Davor were snoozing in their birdcage. (When the baby arrived, they would never have such an opportunity again.) I had got engrossed in reading *The Dream Book* and comparing the interpretations of dreams with the images on the walls of my coffee cup. My about-to-be-dried-up future indicated visitors. Then destiny knocked on the still locked door of the museum.

Everyone knew that Brkić would go to open it. I was expecting Mrs. Flintstone, who was giving me a course in the cuppabet (after Latin, the most widespread script used in our country), but the shadow on our table of rosewood and ivory fell from a different source. Julio and a gentleman whom Julio addressed as Commander approached us.

The gentleman greeted all present, having waited for Dad to wipe the lather from his face. That intermezzo gave me time to commit to memory the following particulars: First, Julio had flung on his newest uniform, black, cut like overalls, with lots of pockets, the exact number of which ranged between seventeen and a hundred and ninety-three, not counting the inside ones. I had already seen such achievements of our local wartime military industry in our sovereign and autonomous market. They reminded me of pilots' or mechanics' uniforms, and the people in them of miners or chimney-sweeps. Over the overalls he wore a waistcoat, which can't have had any fewer pockets. I think that most of the fighters in the city have more pockets than bullets.

While they were waiting for Dad, Julio bent to one side, as though he were doing a yoga pose. Finally, out of a pocket on his knee, he took a lighter. Then he scratched his back, at least that's what it looked like, and took out a pack of Marlboro. He took a cigarette out of one packet and lit it, leaving all the rest as though by chance on the gas cylinder.

Dad, with the face of a child's bottom, finally approached to ask the early visitor the reason for the early visit. Instead of the early visitor, it was Julio who replied: The reason for the early visit was the report that fifth columnists were hiding in the museum.

Like all stupidities, this one wasn't naive, and Dad, knowing that, took a serious interest in the case: What report was this?

It had been reported that someone in the museum was sending messages to the Aggressor.

What?

Various pieces of information.

As Director of the museum, Dad had to reject such a thing. He was the only person who had all the keys, he had accreditation, no one could . . .

But could someone be hiding here, for instance?

For instance, where?

Among them, for instance.

Categorically not!

Did Dad know a Davor such and such?

Yes.

Where did he live?

Why?

Had he responded to his mobilization papers?

Dad said no, and Mother yes. Then Dad backed up Mother's yes, and Mother Dad's no. Then Mother hastened to explain: No, because he worked for the Radio.

They had information, however, that Davor such and such was no longer fulfilling his obligations in keeping with the law. The Commander wished to speak to him.

What about?

About his summons to the Armed Forces.

Davor was a writer. His weapon was the pen.

Pens wouldn't drive tanks away. Would they call him?

He wasn't here. He had gone . . .

Poor Mother. People who don't know how to lie ought to be pensioned off. However, Julio had already offered to bring the escapee, the deserter, the fifth-columnist, the spy . . . He went straight to the birdcage.

Sanja was sitting alone. The place beside her, on the bed, was still warm. Then Julio established that there were neither slippers nor pajamas to be seen, that Davor's sweater was hanging over his trousers on the back of a chair: The suspect had left at most five minutes ago.

Through the window?

Impossible. The window was boarded up.

Was there another way out?

Dad showed them his keys: The other way out was locked.

So, Davor was at this moment in a cage, and more than one person was interested in clipping his wings. The commander whistled, and two more gentlemen came into the museum. I remembered that they had already been our guests. They went through the atrium and began to search the rooms. Dad followed them, helpfully unlocking the locked doors. Julio, on the other hand, scampered ahead of them, scrutinizing the passages and stairs, to catch the fugitive as he slunk from one hiding place to another.

Sanja had got up and remained standing in the doorway of her canton. Brkić had wrapped a sweater round her shoulders, but I don't think she registered it. (I had already noticed this partiality, which had been still more marked since Granny's death and was already obvious to everyone.) She was standing, framed in the doorway, in the pose of a Pietà who, instead of the denounced Jesus, was hugging herself. Some people amaze one with their ability to experience and suffer other people's misfortunes and ill fates as their own.

Julio was scampering increasingly rapidly and his face was acquiring an expression of idiotic confusion. That expression, to a lesser degree, was shared by the others as well. It was all beginning to look like a wedding without the bridegroom. When the errand boy approached Sanja and Brkić, to search the birdcage once more, he stopped instantly, and, as though remembering something, glanced at his Partizan colleague.

The answer to that glance came in the form of a half-threatening, half-mocking attack of coughing. If this had been translated into dialogue, it would have looked like this: Is he in the museum? Yes. You know where he is. Yes, and it would be better for you to go on not knowing.

The leader of the round-up approached as well. He stopped right beside me. He had eyebrows the size of an average mustache, and a mustache the size of an average broom. I was able to confirm the assumption that he first attained six foot in height and only then learned the basic rules of grammar: Eiver 'e's 'ere, in ve museum, so search all ve rooms, or we give it up as a bad job. If he ain't 'ere, it's not my problem. Ve council has ve summons, a courier can give it to 'im.

But they went on nevertheless. They searched both the cellar and the upper floor carefully. I followed them, to scream or do something similar if required. I must admit that they didn't kick the doors. The Quisling must have told them that Davor wasn't dangerous. They peered under the beds, first one of them, then Julio, just in case. They looked behind curtains, opened cupboards, shook the chains on large chests, peered behind the frames of wide canvases. I must acknowledge their speed and thoroughness. The noose around Davor was tightening. I assumed that he was upstairs. We went up there. It was brighter, because the light crumbled into the corridors from the edges of the holes in the roof, and also several windows facing the atrium were open. Now I, too, was becoming curious. Where was Davor?

He wasn't in the toilet. Nor was he in the room with the books. He was not in the Jewish apothecary's. They unrolled two rugs, he wasn't there. In the ethnographic collection three lads were drinking coffee, a girl was embroidering her dowry, another was looking longingly through a latticed window. In the room with the stuffed animals, they tapped on the bear, nothing. Julio and the commander (he had the same surname as Mrs. Flintstone!) were becoming increasingly edgy. Finally, all that was left were the broom cupboard and the ladder to the attic. He wasn't among the brooms. (Maybe because there weren't any brooms, either. Julio had sold them all, because, since there had been no power, they were more expensive than vacuum cleaners.) Finally, the attic.

One of the two climbed up. Julio held his heels. The attic, completely in keeping with the absurdity of war, was the brightest. The holes in the roof shone like angels from the dome of the Sistine Chapel. (I hadn't been there, this is *licentia poetica*.)

But Davor wasn't there. Nor was he on the roof, nor behind the chimney, nor had he jumped.

At last they left.

Brkić went with them, holding Julio back. Sanja went back to her room and to bed. Mother went to the kitchen, after she had looked at Dad for half a minute. He followed her, with lowered eyes.

Had he been obliged to allow this search?

Might makes right.

In this museum, among the paintings, books, and all that past, he was the one who had to be the might.

He hadn't thought it was so dangerous. He knew the commander, he was their neighbor, Mrs. Flintstone's husband!! The two exclamation points are the punctuation marks of my surprise.

And if they had taken Davor away?

They wouldn't have.

People disappear. There are all sorts of stories.

That's right. There are all sorts of stories.

Davor was her son . . .

They behaved correctly. And sometime Davor must grow up.

Why?

Because of her. Because of them. Because of Sanja. Because of the museum . . .

Would he be capable of reporting Davor so that they'd leave his museum alone?

At that question, Dad did not lower his eyes, and I was pleased about that. But he would not reply to such a question. And, of course, as soon as she had uttered it, Mother regretted it. This had nothing to do with Dad.

But how astonished I was when I discovered that it did! I heard him attacking Julio: Out of the question!

Why? They had made an agreement.

To teach Davor a lesson, but not to terrify the pregnant woman and make him quarrel with his wife!

When I had fitted all the little pieces together, the background to this event was as follows. Dad and Julio had arranged to frighten Davor. Julio had brought his fellow-fighters. They were going to pretend to arrest Davor, accusing him of cowardice and faintheart-edness, and then Dad would intervene, promise in Davor's name that he would place himself at the disposal of the Armed Forces. For his role, and for the whole idea, because this was just like him, Julio was to get several parcels of books about Sarajevo. An old and rare edition, because it was published by the museum and sold outside the network of bookshops. Davor had once said of that book that it would now sell like hotcakes. It seemed that Sarajevo was becoming popular in the world, like the works of a dying painter. Or a can with Coca-Cola written on it. Maybe its future coat of arms would be the mark for pure fleece wool.

However, Julio's plans were once again stymied by Brkić. He had prepared Davor for similar campaigns, and developed a plan for urgent evacuation. The nicest thing about the whole episode came at the end. Where had Davor hidden? Julio had been looking at him and not seen him. And I had looked at him, and not recognized him. But Dad must have known that it was him. But still he said nothing.

Baggy trousers, head-scarf, veil . . .

The mannequin looking through the latticed window.

To punish himself for his failure, Dad gave himself a moral slap in the face by voluntarily reporting to a work unit. He went that night to dig, not a tunnyel but trenches. That was a job for several nights, so that he won't be here for the next two. They work at night, because in daylight the Serbs can see the workers and aim at them with snipers or shells.

■ □ ■ □ ■

CHAPTER NINE

Shakespeare. Two creepers. The parachute. How Mother dusted Julio down. A beer bottle. The Women's Antiswine Front.

THE DAY OF BRKIĆ'S DEPARTURE IS GETTING CLOSER. PERHAPS I shall sit up with him for another night or two, in the porter's lodge, with the stove he made from the old boiler. I'll drink cocoa from the lunch packet and watch him making bread: taking the gilded crusts from the hot tin and removing the burned crumbs from them as though caressing each one.

We don't usually talk, just listen to the transistor. But not to the news, like Dad and Davor, or music, like me and Sanja. Brkić can sometimes spend hours twiddling the dial and choosing stations on the medium waves. Languages merge together—English, Chinese, Latin, Hungarian, Italian opera, and the Beatles . . . Sometimes he hears something, a song, a name, or a word, and then he talks about his village and his childhood. I think we all carry in ourselves something like a little fireplace, a picture studded with sun, the memory of a place, or a day, when we were happy and loved, and when the life that lay before us seemed like a tamed and saddled unicorn.

Then Julio burst in, sat down, turned out seventeen pockets until he found a packet of cigarettes, and put it on the top of the heap of bits and pieces he had already extracted: lighters, matches, batteries, pills, bullets, small packets of pepper, a little pack of Vegeta seasoning, condoms, or, as he calls them, "macs." When something catches his attention, he remembers that he might be able to make someone a gift of it, and delivers the pills to Sanja, toothpaste to Davor, razor blades to Dad, a dozen sugar lumps to me, for coffee. (I made the fatal mistake of putting them into a bowl and leaving it on the table.) Finally, in an inner pocket of his waistcoat he found the reason for taking out everything else: a fishing rod, a so-called periscope. The parts are drawn out of each other, so that a yard in length grows into six. Brkić had decoded it even before he saw the label: a Shakespeare! That one word contained excitement and joy and surprise and gratitude. It denoted far more than the name of the author of *Much Ado About Nothing*, it was the name of the factory of this piscatorial scourge of God. (Despite all of this, a Shakespeare is not the best kind of rod. For instance, those made by the DAM factory are better. But a Shakespeare is for Brkić what Tuti-fruti chocolate is for me. Milka, Nestlé, and Toblerone are better. But Tuti-fruti is not merely chocolate. It's a ritual.) I also learned that for bait people use feathers from cockerels' necks, in quest of which Brkić used once, and only for that reason, to travel to Romania. It seems that those feathers are for trout what Tuti-fruti is for me.

When Davor joined us, to listen to the news broadcast by the Serbs, Julio warned him never to dream of having an X-ray.

Why?

It would reveal the Chetniks in his heart.

Davor was angry. By way of defense, Julio mentioned Davor's plan for escaping from the city. I transformed myself into a spy plane.

According to Davor, there are several ways of getting out of the cauldron known as the Bosnian hotpot, Sarajevo. The first is by plane. Expensive, but quickest and safest. The airplane spits the wealthy Sarajevan out in Zagreb. For Davor, however, with his surname, Zagreb is not Europe enough. For names like his there is another way. By Unprofor transporter, into the Serbian side of the city. If Sarajevo is the pot, the Serbian part of the city is the lid. Davor thinks, if one has to be cooked, then it's easier to evaporate from the lid than the bottom. In other words, if he runs away from this army's rifles he'll get the other one's field guns. Brkić: You haven't escaped if you're hiding from the Ustashas among the Chetniks.

Davor knows all of that. But if he has to use a rifle butt to nail his name-plate to the door of some place in the sun . . .

Then isn't it better to do it where there are lots of nails?

No. Where he won't be suspect.

Davor is an intellectual. He will be suspect wherever he goes. And it doesn't suit a man who is expecting a child to behave like a child. There's a war on, let him take a rifle, and heaven knows there are people to aim it at.

His nation?

What is a nation? Sheep droppings in a meadow, which think they are some kind of path.

Since when has Davor been attached to some nation? (This question was directed to him by his wife, later.) Had they not both chosen not to have any allegiance? To be citizens of the world?

Yes, but, in fact, it's not a matter of choice. You are what your father is. That's the simplest way. He wasn't the one who dreamed this up. But that was why he wanted to get out. He had friends there, connections, his father could help him . . .

She wasn't in a position to travel.

Julio had sorted it all. Gas, a driver, a connection in Unprofor.

She shouldn't travel.

She shouldn't sit in a cellar, shaking with the foundations.

There was a hospital here . . .

Destroyed.

Incubators . . .

Switched off.

There's ultrasound here.

There are doctors there.

She felt that it would be better for her to stay. He should do as he wished.

It would be easier to shift the Statue of Liberty than the monolith of my sister-in-law. She is like a tragic hero in classical drama. Once she has decided something, she is prepared for Davor to take all the consequences of her decision. She has wound herself round my brother like a creeper round a stick. Or, better still, the two of them are like two creepers which stay upright by clutching and wrapping themselves round each other. Love is stronger than gravity.

For instance, love of sugar made Sniffy exploit the tone of the dialogue and seriousness of the topic to thrust his nose into the bowl of sugar lumps. My scream saved only two. Davor leapt up, grabbed him by the scruff of his neck, lifted him up, hit him, once, then once again. Then he pushed his nose into the remaining sugar and began to beat him with his belt. He beat him on the back, head, legs, repeating with every blow bad, bad, bad. At first, aware of his sin and guilt, Sniffy bowed his head, half-kneeling, his tail between his legs and ears pressed against his head. Then he began to whine and tremble, but the firm grip didn't allow him to get away. When, from pain or terror, trying to escape the blows, he peed on the rug, Davor went into orbit. He thrust his nose into the puddle, beat him against the wall and furniture, twisted and pinched the skin on his neck, swore and hissed, repeating over and over again bad, bad, bad dog. Sniffy struggled, yelped out loud, turned his head trying to bite the hand at the nape of his neck, while Davor beat him again and again. And then suddenly stopped. Sniffy slipped under the table and lay there trembling, watching Davor with huge, frantic eyes. Davor knelt down and found a rag to wipe up the puddle, then gathered up the spilt sugar with his hand. Then he buried his face in his hands and began to sob. Sanja knelt beside him and pressed him up against her. Sniffy came out from under the table and began to nuzzle his head between them.

Before this war made him into an ordinary creeper, Davor had been a magic beanstalk. He was capable of growing upwards through all the mists and clouds, but now he was withering before our eyes, and soon the only thing about the creeper that would be of any use would be the stick. That's probably why I wrote that word a moment ago. His smile is bitter, he stops rigid halfway through an action, his expression is slow and troubled, his nerves taut, his voice low and unsure, almost sniveling. He is happiest saying nothing, waiting for time to pass and others to leave him alone.

I think I've been quite wrong up to now, attributing his weaknesses to Sanja. And in her I overlook all the things I search for in vain in Davor. Five years ago Sanja's mother fell ill. Sanja went to the hospital twice a day, to bathe her and change her clothes. Then when they brought her home, cured of all attempts at further treatment, Sanja sat by her bedside, turned her over at night, massaged her back, which was sore from lying. She kept repeating to herself that her mother wouldn't and couldn't die. Then she died. Everyone wept, and everyone was relieved, because with time a lengthy and painful death, especially someone else's, becomes a disagreeable obligation and useless labor.

She met my brother and accepted his hand like a blind person who had not intended to cross the road. Davor, full of life and faith in love, convinced her that everything would be as it was before. She said it wouldn't be, that it would never be as it was before. Then she fell pregnant. That was two years ago.

I know why Mrs. Flintstone doesn't immediately reply, when someone says good morning to her. She interrogates herself, just in case she's fallen out with the person in question. She's the most important reason why I call this fictionalized chronicle of mine *The Museum in the Mahala*. Her best friend is Sanja. She doesn't speak to Mother. In fact, that's all Julio's fault, but it suits her better to be angry with Mother. Her morning visit had the purpose of reconnaissance. Instead of leaves and twigs, the scout camouflaged himself with a cloud of steam rising from a pan and smelling of veal soup with carrots and potato. When I saw the privileges and treats enjoyed by an expectant mother, just because she was pregnant, I felt that I ought to modify my resistance to questions of sex and reproduction, and accept immaculate conception.

While still at the door, Mrs. Flintstone asked Sniffy where his master, Davor, was. She hadn't seen him lately. He didn't take the doggy out anymore.

Instead of Sniffy, Sanja answered: Davor was working. He slept at the Radio.

She didn't hear his name in the broadcasts. And she would have recognized him, he had a really photogenic voice.

It's something that's still being recorded. It hasn't been broadcast. Sanja's not particularly interested.

That's not good. He might find someone who is interested. Especially now she's pregnant. He's a man, useless. He'll go looking somewhere else . . . And she'd spent an hour that morning cleaning up mess from the street, and she was surprised he wasn't around. The dogs made messes everywhere, and the kids brought it in on their slippers, and the Persian rug in the hall was completely new. Her Junuz had taken off his boots yesterday. She had washed his socks, they still smelled the same . . . Since he stepped in it. Did Sanja have any cigarettes? (With Fata, it was always like that. You never know whether she's come because of Davor, the mess, or cigarettes.) No.

At that moment the thermometer popped out from under Sanja's armpit. Sanja read out the value of her seventh-this-morning taking of her temperature. I remember my interest in this miracle of technology, so I was not surprised by Fata's reaction. She had already stood up to leave, but she sat down again: Shouldn't it be shaken?

No. It had a button.

Where did she get it from?

A present from Julio.

Proud that it was she, first of the Flintstone dynasty, who had the honor of taking her temperature with a calculator, the wife of Junuz-bey did not know how to thank her and she revealed to Sanja what I had assumed: She knew that Davor was hiding in the museum. Her Junuz had told her.

And how did he know?

He was here yesterday. He was called by the Director and Julio. It would be better for Davor to be mobilized into Junuz's unit, rather than anyone else's.

When our neighbor left, Sanja reported the case to Mother. Mother, of course, couldn't believe it. But by the time Julio initiated a conversation on that theme, her swamis had enlightened her.

Julio: He had talked to his commander, Junuz, asking him to take Davor into his unit. He would give him papers and accreditation, as though he had been mobilized from the beginning of the war.

Why was Julio telling Mother this and not Davor?

Because Davor wouldn't hear of it.

Or because Davor didn't have the money to pay for it. Did the gentleman think that all of us in the museum were idiots? That we couldn't see what he was up to! Did he think that human destinies were the same as coffee and gas? What gave him the right to bring the police into the museum and report her son?

It wasn't him . . .

Was there anything in the world he thought couldn't be traded? Or was everything for sale? He was a serious man, but he behaved like a child. If he had wanted to see what was in the suitcase, why had he not simply asked? And why did he want to know in any case? Was he accustomed to getting everything he wanted? Mother could only tell him that he was on the wrong track. The world of material things was an illusion. He was old, it was time for him to turn to spiritual values. Good could be done without asking or expecting something in return.

Mother went on glowing for some time, like a teacher over a lost pupil for whom there was still hope that he would reform. When she had finished and asked Julio if he really wanted to have Granny's suitcase, he got up embarrassed, bowed, and went out. He had been dusted down, like dust beaten out of an old carpet. Mother had shaken out of him long years of accumulated layers of insolence, greed, and effrontery. At least she was convinced she had. Unfortunately, dust quickly returns to old carpets, sometimes even more quickly than it was beaten out. At lunch he said something to the effect that it would be cleverer for Davor to be plugged in. (Plugged in. As though people were electrical apparatus, and state politics electricity.)

For Sanja, Brkić would have been prepared to pour a whole beer bottle full of blood out of his own veins. But destiny devises cruel jokes. Sanja came with an empty bottle, not for blood, however, but—for alcohol: it was high time the toilet was disinfected. As far as the history of art is concerned, Sanja now looked less like the Pietà, and more like Botticelli's Venus, holding her stomach with one hand, so that the baby wouldn't fall out if the knot on her womb gave way and unraveled.

Davor, of course, could not allow the expectant one to do that. He took the bottle from her, and left picking up Sniffy's moltings for later. While he was looking for rubber gloves, Dad, who was not au fait with the situation, appeared with the newspaper and occupied the cubicle. Three minutes later he came out with tears in his eyes. I thought that he had read something sad in the paper, but then Davor came back, went into the cubicle, and came out again immediately, turning the empty bottle in his hands. He asked us whether a bottle of alcohol could evaporate in three minutes.

In the end, Sanja was angry with Davor, because he never finished what he had begun, and Dad was angry with Mother because she hadn't warned him. It seems that people as a rule get angry with the people they're used to and not with the person who is really to blame. So Brkić was angry with Julio because he had taken one of the two pints of methyl alcohol in the cellar in an unknown direction, and now they hadn't a drop left.

Julio, a pupil of dialectical materialism, couldn't see anything terrible in the fact that he gave one thing to one person today, to another tomorrow, and to a third the day after tomorrow. He did it in order to please as many people as possible. And he didn't understand why almost the same number remained disappointed or angry. For instance, he had given Mother a sack of hazelnuts. Mother hadn't had a chance to recover from her enthusiasm, when Julio exchanged the hazelnuts for coffee. He had given Sanja a box of powdered milk, and then taken that same box to the children's hospital. And his justifications were poetry. When he had taken away the baby spoons, which he had also previously given to Sanja, that was so as not to put a jinx on Sanja so that later she wouldn't have milk. When he took away our gas masks, that was so as not to bring down some ill on our heads.

Brkić has a new hobby. With his beloved Shakespeare he throws lead and fish-hooks into pots and jugs on the other side of the atrium. As he does so, he listens to Julio's explanation of recent events. It goes like this: He, Julio, isn't even this guilty. He only connected the interested parties. The Director had wanted to give Davor a bit of a fright, to give us all something to think about. It wasn't remotely funny to share the cellar with a deserter and military refugee. And the commander had long ago wanted to see whether his headquarters could be moved into the museum. But he didn't want the Director to know about that, until it became official. Why worry the man in advance?

May she come in and would she be disturbing anybody, Mrs. Flint-stone arrived, scurrying after her nose. Some women's ears remind one of wings. In fact, some women's whole appearance reminds one of birds: a small head on a long neck, tiny eyes, a pointed, thin, and hooked nose, like a beak. Why had she come at this late hour?

She'd brought Sanja a bit of pie and potato, her Junuz had brought it from the terrain. And she'd come to tell us that we didn't have to give the oil back. And she'd come to ask the Doctor something, but she could ask Julio something as well, since he was here. Could her neighbor, Julio, somehow manage to buy her a ther-mometer? She'd pay. (As though one could buy something without paying.)

What sort?

What sorts are there?

The same as Sanja's. With music. Modern. Newly composed. Ceca Veličković. It measures your weight and blood pressure as well. And tells the time. It even has an alarm.

Mrs. Flintstone doesn't think that sounds possible. Julio tells all kinds of tall stories, but you never know with a calculator. The only thing that bothers her is the music. If it was someone else, and not Ceca: Did they come with any other music?

Julio didn't think they did. The ones he brought had been left by the Chetniks, like surprise mines. He'd look to see whether there were any with operas. They were dropped by the allies from air-planes.

The Parachute Campaygne

I'm crouching in a bush, reading a Russian detective story. Some student's planning to kill an old woman with an axe and rob her. And just as he raises his arm, someone behind me discharges his personal weapon. Whoever he is, a courier, he laughs at my alarm, he's been sent for me, they're looking for volunteers. I don't know which is worse: that he won't let me find out what happened to the old woman, or that I've shit on my rucksack. In such and such a headquarters, there's a parachute campaygne. The allies are drop-ping humanitarian aid, and I'm to light a fire on a patch of waste ground and collect whatever falls there. That's what I does. The fire flares and planes start buzzing from all directions, like mosquitoes. There's parachutes like dandelion seeds after someone's blown on it. And one comes straight for me. I dashes left, it comes left, I dashes right, it comes right, I jumps into a stream, it falls into the stream. If I hadn't rapidly dug myself a trench, it would've flattened me in the middle of that meadow. There's three bales on the palette. One has burst, boots are falling out of it. Brand new, NATO-Pact originals. But all reject goods. You couldn't find a matching pair to save your life. Either they're not the same size or they're both right, or both left. I abandons the hopeless business and examines the second bale. It's full of tin cans. I opens them, they contain cookies. Hungry, I takes one. Crack, my tooth snaps as though made of glass, not porcelain. I bites harder, crack again, my plate snaps in half. I digs my heels in. I takes my knife, and, using the serrated edge, I saws and files, the edge loses its teeth, but the cookie's untouched. Then I starts shoving them in my pockets, but just you try to fill them. If there's one pocket in my overalls, there's fifty. I examines the third bale as well. It's full of sleeping bags, feathery, feathers from Christmas turkeys. When they're packed, they fit into a pocket, and when they're opened out, they're like a haystack. I shoves them into my pockets as well, I keep thinking the feathers are rustling, until I look round. Fifty yards from me a tank with a silencer has sneaked up on me. And it's firing a burst of shells straight at me. Thanks to the cookies in my pockets, the pellets bounce off it like a bulletproof vest. I leaps behind the bale full of feathery bags, a burst of fire into the bags, feathers fly all over the meadow. The firing stops. I peers out from behind a boot, they've got out of the tank, thinking it's snowing, and are putting chains on the caterpillar treads. But the chains have been washed at several hundred degrees and shrunk, they simply can't get them on. At headquarters, no one believes the story about the cookies. I reaches in my pocket, but the shells have pulverized them. Whenever someone taps me on the shoulder, out fly feathers on one side of me and dust on the other.

Our neighbor was bored by Julio's stories. She could hardly wait for the end and me to take her to Dad. He was in the library, preparing pictures for the transporter. I said that I was looking for a book, so he wasn't suspicious about me staying, and, leafing through *The Lexicon of the People's Heroes of the National Liberation War,* I heard an interesting conversation.

Before I reproduce it, I should describe the library: in it the books are not arranged as in other similar places, but one on top of the other, from the floor as high as possible, like columns. Dust falls on them, and through the slits in the boards nailed over the windows, swords of light pierce them. If anyone saw this on a film, he would think that the scene took place in an attic. So, Mrs. Flintstone greeted Dad: *Merhaba,* neighbor.

Buryum. (Recently Dad has been speaking two languages in parallel. When I drew Mother's attention to this, she explained that the new language was, in fact, the language of his childhood, that's how his grandma, grandpa, and uncle spoke. And as far as the greetings themselves were concerned, they were gradually replacing accreditation. There were so many greetings that they not only separated one faith from another, but one conviction from another. For example, former communists, who had become old believers overnight, on leaving said *Poselam* and *ciao.* Dad says that they were once commies, and now they're "sommies." That expression derives from the word *somun* which denotes a kind of loaf, round, flat, and slit on top. *Somun* is the favorite bread of Muslim believers during their fast called Ramadan.)

Unsure how to begin, Mrs. Flintstone picked up a book entitled *Good Morning, Belgrade.* It'll be Good Night for them as well, God willing. Then she took Bašeskija's *Chronicle* from another column, saw that it wasn't a book about chronic complaints, and then finally got down to it. It wasn't on her own account. Her Junuz brought chicken and beef to them. But there were people who got only pig. Whatever they opened, there was ham and pork in them.

Was our neighbor talking about the lunch packets?

Yes. What did the Doctor think about it?

Aid was aid. People sent what they could. If someone didn't eat it, he could exchange it.

They'd thought of refusing it. Telling the local authority not to accept it anymore. There was fish, there was feta cheese . . .

There was no coffee, matches, fruit juices, or sweets. Or toilet paper.

There was water; people hadn't used paper before the war, either.

There wasn't any water. Cars didn't bring barrels right to everyone's door.

And there wouldn't be either, as long as he was sitting in the cellar. Her Junuz had risked his neck on three front lines to take canisters of gas out of Chetnik garages. (If that's the case, he was wrong. In the city itself there was a closer and less risky bore-hole. It was called Unprofor. And she could ask Davor for several locations.)

That was the end of Dad's conversation with the representative of the initiative committee of the Women's Antiswine Front, which had launched the initiative of refusing further aid in the form of lunch packets because of the high concentration of pork in the bacon.

And as far as the canisters of oil were concerned, they weren't dragged away from the front line, but bought in the middle of town, in the barracks occupied by soldiers of the United Nations, by nationality Ukrainians, I believe. So much for that.

■ □ ■ □ ■

CHAPTER TEN

Alice in Canisterland. What Julio sat through the night on. Vitamin C.
Scratching the bear.

THE HIGHLIGHT OF THE DAY, WEEK, FORTNIGHT, MONTH, WAS
going for water, to the Vekil-Harčov Mosque. Since I had envisaged
describing that scene in the form of a lyric description appropriate
for a stayologue, I have waited for suitable conditions and inspiration, which I consider to prevail in this early morning, in the
porter's lodge, beside a large cup of white chicory.

We put ten five-liter canisters onto the cart Brkić had made. The
cart was constructed out of two wheels from a child's bicycle and
the supports for a ready-made bookshelf. Only Brkić and I went. I
was humming an old folk song: In a jug I catch water sweet, then to
the cellar to rinse my feet.

When I went that afternoon with Brkić for water, to the fountain at
the Vekil-Harčov Mosque, known as Hadžijska, I saw a parked car
in front of the Palace of the United Flintstones. It had an American
registration plate, with Junuz written on it. The car was tied, like a
dog, to the courtyard by a wire. I assumed (correctly!) that it was an
alarm system.

The mornings were already becoming a little fresher. The Viewpoint on Trebević mountain (once a restaurant with a view over
most of the city, and now an artillery position with the same view)
was puffing the mist away. Stray dogs rooted in the heaps of garbage
that had sprung up on the erstwhile taxi-ranks. Out of windows

poked cooking stoves and out of them, beside the sooty walls, wound black columns of smoke.

Canisters with bent people ran across the wide streets and cross-roads. Brkić walked slowly. I liked the fact that he didn't drive me to walk along the inside edge, or in the shadow, either. Suddenly, as in the film *The Name of the Rose*, the Vijećnica loomed up in front of us. The outside walls were still there, and the holes in them that had once been windows. On the top the decorations still stood, crosses and fleurs-de-lis. The building, without the glass in which for a whole century Sarajevo, Trebević, and the sky had been reflected, reminded one of the face of a person with the eyes gouged out. As we drew nearer, I could see the interior through those holes. The ceilings and floors had collapsed, and where there had once been a tiled hall, now there was an enormous heap of burnt beams, iron pipes, and sooty bricks. Inside, out of the walls, like shells on a rock or fungus on a tree-trunk, pieces of staircase hung over that heap, no longer leading anywhere or coming from anywhere. And over everything, like black butterflies, trembled and hovered the burned pages of books and blackened cards from the catalog.

When you got quite close, through the ground-floor windows, through which it had once been impossible to see anything, the sky was now visible. Under those windows, there was a truck with TD B&H written on it, into which people were loading coal from the Vijećnica cellar. Old people and women with bags, baskets, and sacks were going in and out of the cellar.

Beyond the burned building, the view opened out onto the Viewpoint. People with canisters and trolleys were running across the bridge over the Miljacka. Brkić hurried a bit, because of me, although he was ill, and he paid for every long stride and abrupt movement with coughing and wheezing. He complained of his lungs, but Mother was afraid that it was actually his heart.

We crossed the bridge and joined one of the four queues for water. That is to say, I joined the queue, while Brkić sat down and lit a cigarette. He did that with two lighters, one of which had gas in it and the other a working flint. Where the four queues were, there were two fountains. There were always two columns for one source. One consisted of people waiting their turn, and the other of those who would try to push in before their turn. Beside each column of people there was also a column of means of transport. People carried water on their backs, on the aluminum frame of rucksacks or cobbled-together packsaddles to which barrels were attached. They dragged water in carts and prams, pushed it in wheelbarrows or trolleys, drove it on bicycles.

The mosque courtyard is surrounded by a high wall, crossed by a stone path and overgrown with clumps of roses and bushes with red leaves, behind which gravestones half sunk in grass peer out. The view from this courtyard, through the lattice of the windows cut into the wall, leaves the impression that everything begins and ends here, and that nothing of all that can be seen outside—not the cobbled street, nor the poplars along the river bank, nor the bridge, nor the burned out Vijećnica—matters. The whole world outside the mosque courtyard, seen through the greasy black grille, looks as though it were in a prison, condemned to destruction and transience. Only within, on this side, where the water can be heard trickling through the scent of the roses, is freedom. I think I have only just realized what point of view is!

After that I listened to the people in the queue for a bit. Some were silent and looked straight ahead, they had not yet begun to believe that all this had happened to them and that here they were, at the end of the twentieth century, in the middle of a city in the middle of Europe, standing, waiting to pour a little water from a rubber tube into plastic containers.

After all I've seen, I'll have to moderate my racist stance toward refugees. Among them are people who were born in this city and who grew up here, and have now fled from their own apartments in the so-called occupied parts of town to the houses of their parents and the rooms of their childhood. They were driven out of their homes by rough threats, harassment, insults, and blows. First bearded, greasy, and drunken men, waving knives, grenades, and golden crosses would come, followed by polite, orderly, shaven men who would shrug their shoulders and advise flight. That is how the Serbs liberated their holy century-old Serbian local authorities, and that is how non-Serbs jumped through their windows and cellars out of their lives into other people's plans and calculations.

They talked about records, badges, materials, patterns, albums, tools, machines . . . As though I had suddenly woken up, I stood and saw that I, too, was a refugee. This is how, sooner or later, everyone will finally wake up. The man behind the red-hot barrel will realize that he has killed children, the man behind God's commandments will discover that he has trampled on every single one of them.

The way home: Children throw stones at an Unprofor transporter. The windows with still unbroken panes are covered with brown sticky tape, so that the explosions don't turn them into dangerous shards. No one looks through them, because all that could be seen would be the place from where the shrapnel would come. Even out of the sky, blue and hazy with the intense heat shimmering over the hot asphalt and red-hot walls of the Vijećnica.

I think about the way carts full of ore turn whoever is pulling them into beasts. On the uphill slope I feel someone helping me by pushing. I turn and see Mirza. He has a sticker on his forehead designed like a large sticking plaster. I ask him what happened, had he not picked up the anti-armored television set properly? And as soon as I had said that, I wanted to sink into the ground with shame. He smiled: They didn't all fight like Julio or Junuz. What did I think, why weren't the Chetniks coming into Sarajevo, as they had into Foča or Višegrad?

Then I asked him some more stupidities, trying to be nice and disguise how uncomfortable I felt, and he answered briefly and in a business-like way. He took the ore from me, dragged the cart right up to the museum door, and went away. The way I write about people and talk to them now seems like pointless and childish goading with paper darts.

Mirza was wounded in an attack. He had attacked and been prepared to kill. He went to kill the Serbs who stood behind the field-gun. (Mortar, anti-aircraft gun, Tommy gun, death-sewer, automatic, repeater, shooter, piece. This is an opportunity for me to boast about my knowledge of the personal weapons of a Serbian soldier.) He went to kill a Chetnik, with greasy hair and a great filthy beard, who was hurling shells and grenades to kill children, women, and old people in the streets, in front of their houses, in their beds. He went to kill Serbian knights who attack first and without warning, kill the unarmed and helpless, rape women, mutilate the wounded, destroy hospitals, and burn books. He asked me whether I was carrying a first-aid bandage with me. What for?

Last night I didn't sleep well. No one did. And not because shells were falling somewhere nearby, we're used to that by now, but because after every earthquake the alarm on Junuz's car went off. I was right about that wire, then; it was used to tether cars like horses once in the Wild West.

The one who suffered most from lack of sleep was Julio. We found him in the morning with a brownish face, like someone recovering from typhus. He was sitting in the porter's lodge on Granny's suitcase! When Brkić and I came in, he stood up, lifted up the suitcase and gave it to me: There, I was a witness, he hadn't opened it. Let Brkić find some other bonehead. Julio hadn't swallowed the hook. They could take the suitcase back.

Brkić said nothing.

Julio sighed, as though a stone the size of the suitcase had fallen from his heart: What had Brkić put into it?

Nothing.

Yes he had. There was something inside. A spring? Old newspapers? Dirty underpants?

Brkić knew nothing about it.

Julio knew him like his own wallet. He had planted something on him. Otherwise why would he have left it in the middle of the table. What had he packed for him?

Mother came in. She saw the suitcase in my arms, was pleased, took it, muttered that she had forgotten to put it away the previous night, and went out with it. Brkić and I followed her.

Julio stayed staring straight in front of him.

When I came later to call him for lunch, I found him in the same position, only now he was talking to himself. Something about returning something with interest.

The walking Ooof had read a book by a doctor—Paulus, or Pauling—in which he had proved the irreplaceable value of vitamin

C. That vitamin was found in fresh fruit and vegetables, but particularly in tablets, for which reason they had to be acquired urgently
and without fail.

Mother tried patiently to explain the yin-yang theory of nutrition
and the absolute harm of taking vitamins in the form of chemical
compounds. There was quite enough in orache . . . Then she picked
a sprig of that tough and bitter herb. Brkić found some unripe
plums, Dad two wilting lemons out of which not even the Gestapo
would have been able to squeeze a teaspoon of juice, but it was only
when Julio appeared, with two plastic jars with a picture of a green
apple on them, under which was written *Irer Apoteke, Grune
Punkte,* that the walking Ooof allowed herself a smile of gratitude.

Each jar contained 100 grams of vitamin C in powder form.

Being pregnant means rubbing your belly instead of an Aladdin's
lamp. One day I'll ask her to give it a rub while wishing that the war
should end. It's worth a try.

Someone had informed Mrs. Flintstone that something had been
brought into the museum, and she appeared while Julio was still
smiling as he received the gratitude of the pregnant young married
couple. The very next instant she had sniffed the white powder, and
then with a gracious grimace admitted that she was immured to
medicines.

Sanja explained that vitamin C was not a medicine but a substitute for fruit.

Yes, beggars can't be choosers and a poor man benefited when
even a fly flew into his arse. Well, her Junuz had brought two
pounds of *insan* coffee. You mix it with sugar, pour hot water over it
and it tastes like the real thing. Her Junuz calls it ekspresso.

Davor didn't think that espresso was the same as instant coffee.

It was all the same. But if you asked her, there was no coffee
without a *džezva.* Was Ramiz-aga in the museum?

She meant my Dad. And she called Mother Ramiz-aginica. I had
noticed that as of a few days ago our neighbors had started using
medieval titles, which is confirmation of the theory that the transi-
tion from socialism to capitalism passes through the Middle Ages. I

would really like to bump into my Serbo-Croato-Bosnian teacher and ask him to explain this phenomenon to me.

He would probably say that it was·a political, and not a linguistic problem, that it wasn't important what a language was called, but that the people who spoke it could understand one another.

And I would reply that he was behaving like an ostrich. He was sticking his head into his books as into a flower pot filled with sand. He had original and charming views on life because his over-reading had prevented him from living. Brkić said that language was to the people the same as a wife to her husband. You liked other people's, but you wouldn't give up your own.

In this country the language has first to be called something, so that people know whether they want to understand it or not.

If I were to use a hidden camera to make a silent film in which Sanja and Mrs. Flintstone exchange experiences, it would look like this: They are sitting down. Then one stands up and knocks on the table three times, from underneath. The other smiles. Then one shifts from her place, more exactly from one side of her behind to the other, and the other does the same thing. They are both deadly serious. From time to time they look up. As rapidly as one talks, the other just as rapidly nods her head. Sanja takes Sniffy's hairs out of Fata's clothes, she waves Sanja away, indicating that it doesn't bother her. I think that you could make a good silent film about our stay in the museum. This whole war is like a burlesque.

The summer is over when people start thinking about winter, says Brkić. This year that happened at the end of spring. The windows on buildings were broken, the roofs of houses had collapsed or had holes in them. Damp nestled comfortably in under the plaster and mortar. Sanja, as a qualified architect, maintained that, if something were not done quickly, all the damaged clay-brick houses would collapse. Fall apart. Melt. And if there were no water, the pipes would freeze and burst. Without electricity, the night would start, as in Sweden, immediately after breakfast.

I remember that once in a class about the art of film, we had the task of writing the scenario for an advertisement. My prize-winning work showed a stable with airplanes, tanks, jeeps, and diggers coming out of it. Then the camera went into the stable, and showed a hen on a nest in the hay, with soldiers, giraffes, horses, and Pink Panthers leaping out from under her. Then the hen squawked, stood up, and in the nest under her there were Kinder Eggs.

Now I would imagine that advertisement like this: artillery pieces, airplanes, cows, soldiers, and Smurfs enter the museum. Then the next image: I am sitting shivering, wrapped in a coat, under which everything that was just shown entering the museum fits. Finally I get up and you see that I have been sitting on a small metal stove, into which I am throwing the toys from Kinder Eggs as fuel.

Dad wrote in his duty notebook the decree that several stoves must not be lit at the same time, and that cooking should be done at the lowest possible heat. The decree also included a list of all the stuff we had up to now considered garbage, but which from now on we had to consider raw material for heating purposes.

I am sitting in the porter's lodge, writing, so as not to forget this morning's chicory which we women drank, with Julio in the title role. Sanja thanked him several times. I also expressed wonder at his altruism. Even Mother, who considers every powder other than *vibhuti* poison, praised Julio's readiness at every moment to do whatever he could. When he had begun to feel a bit uncomfortable, he admitted that it was not his doing, but Brkić's. For two jars of vitamin C, Julio had to donate a pistol. And not any old pistol, but a trophy, with an engraved coat of arms, dedication, date, factory emblem . . . In short, Brkić's wartime pistol. In the city, according to Davor, pistols were like cars in Hollywood. Old-timers were the rage. One stratum of defenders of the city had already made a profit with which they could buy the most expensive and most up-to-date models, and now sixty-year-old trophy guns had increased in value.

Julio quickly passed over this, and then asked Mother whether she had checked that everything that had been in the suitcase was there.

Yes.

He hadn't even opened it.

She didn't doubt that. Julio was a gentleman, polite, honest, and above all Granny's devoted friend.

The memory of that respected lady lay on his heart. He didn't know what was in it, but it must be something valuable. Had Mother thought of keeping the suitcase in the museum safe?

The safe was full of the museum's precious possessions.

But it would still be better if it were properly secured.

Mother had already talked it over with Mr. Brkić. He was going to put the suitcase in a safe place.

That was an excellent solution. There's no doubt that that would be a very secure place.

Someone knocked at the door. This is why I'm never going to finish what I begin to note down and why this cannot be either a novel or a diary. A novel can't be written when someone keeps interrupting you while you are making an effort not to write a diary. And I am making an effort not to write a diary, because now every salesperson in the market is writing one.

Brkić did not after all fly off in his balloon, as planned. The heap of rags remained a heap of rags, because there were no gas cylinders to breathe life into them. And this is why there weren't.

The knock at the door, because of which I had interrupted my writing, was the doing of commander Junuz, with his assistant, Clarence. So I went and opened the door.

Was Julio in the museum?

Yes.

Commander Junuz was angry. I led him into the kitchen, but Julio was not there. We eventually found him in the cellar, with a candle held above his head and his nose pressed against the wall.

What was he doing in the cellar?

Just checking the walls, to see if there were any cracks and so on . . .

Did he know who had promised his Fata a thermometer?

Yes, but . . .

A digital one, it measured the blood pressure, played Halid and Hanka, gave the right time, the numbers of telephone subscribers . . .

That was a joke.

Let him joke with his mother, but let him dmn well not take the fckng pss out of his wife (the censor has left the vowels out of some words). And he'd fckd him over that raid. Were those cylinders full? (He pointed to the four gas cylinders.)

Yes, but . . .

Clarence was already unscrewing Brkić's burners from them and taking the bottles away. If he were ever left without weapons or ammunition, he would continue to impale the enemy on his defiantly stuck-out chin. Mother had heard the commotion and came down to ask whether she could help in any way.

Yes, she could. She should tell the respected doctor that they were satisfied with the state of the museum, and that they would be moving the headquarters there in a few days' time. They were requisitioning the gas for the people's kitchen. They'd be getting a receipt, a stamp with fleurs-de-lis. *Allahimanet.*

When they had gone, I went to look for Dad and Brkić. They were upstairs packing exhibits into wooden packing cases. Brkić cursed Julio out loud, and Dad the authorities to himself. Of course, they stopped what they were doing. Dad went immediately to the Ministry and several headquarters, while Brkić soon appeared in the porter's lodge dressed in his Partizan jacket, with a silver Turkish musket in his hand. He ordered Julio to lead him to Junuz's headquarters.

It would be better for him not to scratch the bear.

And for the arsehole to shift his butt.

Brkić was really angry. They went out. I heard Julio explaining something. He came back for a brief moment, put the musket down, and went out again.

After an hour they were back in the museum, each with one gas cylinder. Brkić was wheezing and as soon as they came in he sat down, gasping for breath. Immediately after them came Dad. They hadn't been able to do anything in the Ministry. Or at Supreme Command, either. If the commander had established that the museum as a building was more suitable for defense, then it was up to the Director to help. Dad then abandoned official demands and moved into friendly connections and convictions. He extracted promises that the matter would be looked into. In the worst case, he would get workers from civil defense to move the exhibits to another location. Namely, in view of military activities, the law and defense plans required that the museum collection be moved to a safer place. Dad hesitated between these two evils. If he decided on saving the cultural treasures, the museum building would be left empty and there would no longer be any practical obstacle to moving into it people who had previously been driven out of it. But if he tried to retain the building, it could very easily happen not only that he did not succeed, but he would be left without a not insignificant number of exhibits. Dad's dilemma could be described like this: He would give his right hand to be right-handed.

In the evening, along came Commander Junuz. With him and automatic rifles came also four warriors. They were looking for Julio again. I said that he had gone out, as he had himself instructed me, before running down to the cellar.

Then Brkić stood in front of me and asked why they were looking for Julio.

To ask him about two bottles of gas.

Were they, perhaps, two of the four that were stolen from here today?

The four warriors shoved their way past us and began to search with their feet through the heap of flags in the atrium. Junuz's attention was also drawn to the five-starred flags and red color. Under the war flags of the Partizan brigades two gas bottles poked out.

What are these flags?

Whatever they are, they're not for being trodden on.

I think that I shall succeed in describing what happened next. Brkić struck a match and set fire first to one and then another rag that were stuffed into the necks of two bottles which he took out of his overalls. The parties winced at this, but they didn't at first believe that there was oil in the bottles. In the meantime, Brkić had taken a grenade out of his pocket, a so-called spoonbill. He took the so-called safety catch off it, in the form of a ring, and hooked it to a button on his jacket.

The young men took a few steps back and raised the barrels of their guns. They looked at Junuz.

He was confused. He had not expected that he would have to shoot anyone because of two gas bottles, especially not someone crazy enough to risk his neck because of them. But he didn't have time to make any kind of decision. Brkić coughed, grabbed his chest, stumbled, caught hold of the doorpost. And the grenade fell into the flags. Everyone rushed out of the atrium into the hall and threw themselves on the floor.

However, the grenade did not explode. Brkić straightened himself, as though he had never coughed in his life, picked up the grenade, and put it into his pocket. And out of his pocket he took the so-called lighter. The part without which the grenade could not explode. Then he extinguished the rags and took them out of the necks of the bottles, closed one of them and poured something out of the other one into six small glasses.

Junuz was standing in the hall doorway. One after another, the lads stood up. Brkić sat down at the table and gestured to Junuz to sit down opposite him. Then he shouted for Julio to come down. I was surprised when he appeared from upstairs, when I had seen him hurtling down into the cellar. Junuz sat down and drained his glass, without taking his eyes off Brkić: What if they had fired?

They hadn't.

But if they had?

Why should they?

Out of fear.

They weren't afraid of him.

In self-defense.

He hadn't attacked them.

Then Junuz smiled: If he had ten men like Brkić, he would liberate Sarajevo. Then he stood up and proposed a toast to him. The lads were still looking at him uncertainly. May as well be hanged for a sheep as a lamb, said Junuz and sent one of them for something better to drink. If it hadn't all happened so fast, he, Junuz, would not have lain on the floor. But he was taken by surprise. Was Brkić seventy?

Somewhere round that.

No one had ever . . . And he coughed, and dropped the grenade . . .

And so it went on, between remorse and admiration, between justification and amazement. I waited for him to stop smiling, to get up and beat the old man up, but life is after all more complicated than a spaghetti western. Brkić had showed that he was not afraid, and it seemed that people like Junuz valued that. And maybe peace was made also because Brkić did not in any way represent competition. And, finally, it seemed, it was possible to learn a great deal from him.

Maybe I'll try again to read the book *How the Steel Was Tempered*.

This postponement of the journey turned out to be a fortunate circumstance. That night between eleven and midnight we had shelling. There were a few innovations. First, they were firing from positions where they had not been before. Second, with so-called heavier weapons. And third, the alarm on Junuz's Golf kept going off and we all prayed that one shell would put paid to the terrified nag. Junuz, however, to spite the enemy, sang, and I managed to make a note of one of the songs: I like to lie with another's wife so lean, and listen to the beating of her spleen.

■ □ ■ □ ■

CHAPTER ELEVEN

Following the nose. De narrator id laid low by a code. Rise, despised of the world. Decorating the bride. *The Book of Changes.* A parcel from Belgrade. Julio's historic contribution to macrobiotics.

TWO MORE NIGHTS PASSED, AND ONLY ON THE THIRD DID THE balloon finally take off. Before I gather in one place the inspiration, talent, and conditions for writing, I shall entertain myself with some short scenes.

First Mrs. Flintstone came with a tray, enveloped in the aroma of real coffee. She had come to ask whether we knew who was the best orthopedist for teeth, because her little girl's jaw had gone crooked. Thank God, her Junuz had a broad-shouldered hand. Junuz had been in action and seized a bottle of gas from the Chetniks, so now she had something to make coffee on. He had brought the children thermal socks as well.

Second, Sniffy ran away. He didn't come home the whole night. Davor and Sanja were beside themselves. I thought that Sanja loved him more, he had guarded her pregnancy on the same bed, but Davor, at the risk of being stopped and mobilized, went out a hundred times, whistling through the *mahalas.* (*Mahala,* a small segment of the city. Larger than a street, but smaller than a munici- pality. If a *mahala* is compared to a flower, the lanes would be the petals, and the mosque the pistil. The inhabitants of the *mahala* behave according to the decrees of a codex which I have not deci- phered in its entirety, but which has these interesting laws: the inhabitant of a *mahala* addresses someone at a window in order to say something to a person beneath the window. The window is, evidently, the trademark of the *mahala*. It is recognized by pots of flowers, an antiblister cushion for the elbows, and a car's rearview mirror for the natural selection of unannounced visitors. The female inhabitants of the *mahala* won't start any job in the kitchen without first looking through one such window. And finally, every sentence must end with the words *mashallah* or Godwilling.) In the morning Sniffy was found in one of the bays in the ocean of garbage. That's called following your nose.

And one night it rained. Until two in the morning, we put buckets, pots, and bowls under streams and torrents of rainwater. That was, apparently, the best water for washing one's hair, and it was also good for boiling clothes. Even if that weren't right, it was good for watering God's gardens where even the emperor walked barefoot. Brobably that ith why by dothe lookth more like a broken tap than an organ-growth behind which by head ith hidden. Mother, of course, trotted out her maxim that every cold is the result of complex processes involving the fullness of the moon, a drop in temperature, the time of year, the humidity of the air, and exaggerated enjoyment of sweets, fruit, milk, and coffee.

And so, while I'm wiping my nose with one handkerchief, and my eyes with another, Julio comes in and informs me that, if I want, I can go that evening with him to the headquarters. The young people were celebrating someone's birthday. I pretended that as well as my nose and eyes, my ears were blocked, too, but Julio was persistent: What should he say, would I come? They're all young people, good-looking, cheerful, it wouldn't do me any harm to go.
     No doubt they'd promised him a reward if he brought me. Danks, I can't, I'b laid low wid a code. I'be got a bigraide.

That same evening, while I was pretending I had forgotten that someone nearby was celebrating some birthday, Mother handed me a small box, with my name written on the cardboard, in handwriting that had gone quite crooked with the effort to be tidy. In the box I found two lemons, three little containers of honey, ten sugar cubes, five camomile tea bags, a pack of aspirin, chocolate, and a little note with get-well-soon wishes. Instead of a signature, in the corner of the piece of paper there was a little picture of a man with a raised hand, probably cut out of a photograph of a Bosnian *stećak*. And pinned to it, a similar earring.

In the letter I'll write to express my gratitude for this gift, I'll suggest to the donor that he seek his happiness at the other end of the rainbow. I am too precocious a soul and like an airplane that crashes after takeoff because its wings think that they can continue to fly by themselves. I know that love is a chemical process, like digestion or sweating. What sugar is in food, love is in reproduction. On the one hand a parcel, a little picture, a guitar, books, but all of that is an illusion, a mist over the whirlpool into which the time has come for the salmon to throw their spawn.

I've still got a cold, and my nose is dripping onto this paper which waits like a challenge. (I've been reading Meša Selimović. Everything is too accurate to be genuine. There is even one piece of wisdom for Davor: Afraid of a trap, afraid of crap, when shall I live?) I am writing in my work place, in the porter's lodge, at the table that is bewitchingly decorated by a bouquet of nineteen roses. The roses protrude from a vase which is, in fact, part of a large shell, a cylinder that from the middle upwards has separated into curls and tongues of unequal length and sharpness. I can guess who it's from and who it's for, especially after Julio couldn't explain how it materialized here, during his shift. He didn't know, he was asleep.

And he had things to rest from. He was supposed to be sending his friend off on a balloon voyage to the center of the earth in eighty days.

The actual ceremony of takeoff consisted of two parts. In the afternoon Julio and Brkić said farewell. They drank, and they were served by a maid of Sarajevo, me. Hence I am in a position to expand my knowledge of the two of them. On the Island in Belgrade, on Brkić's barge, there was a lot of good drink. For example, you drank sitting on chairs, but in water up to your chest, so that you didn't have to go to the toilet every five minutes. Once they put a rubber snake into a handbag belonging to a lady Julio was chatting up. She began shrieking for Julio to come, grab the snake heroically by the throat and hurl it into the Sava River. Everything went well and according to plan, until Julio realized that what he had in his hand was not rubber but something cold and slippery, ugh. It took five minutes of slapping to bring him round. The lady tried hardest.

A night without clouds, moonlight, or stars had drawn over itself the veil of today's smoke and tomorrow's dew. In the courtyard were Davor, Julio, Brkić, and me. Dad had gone to bed. He didn't believe that this whole higgledy-piggledy hodge-podge would take off. Mother had agreed to take my place in the porter's lodge, and Sanja was sulking because Brkić had pigheadedly refused not to make a fool of himself.

We had already grown used to the hissing of the gas. The balloon was nearly full. The five-pointed stars, hammers and sickles, where there were any, looked like patches. Instead of an advertisement for Coca-Cola, it said ETINU DLROW EHT FO SNAIRATELORP.

Davor was whistling, and he infected me, and I began to sing as well: Flee from us, nocturnal shades, our time has come. Down with power and injustice . . .

The basket itself, in the shape of a cube, was made of boards. From its sides hung Gavrilo Princip, Žerajić, and two other bronze heads in the function of ballast. The ropes were fairly taut and from time to time we heard a creak. Brkić stepped down into the basket from the side of the well. Julio took Brkić's pistol out of his pocket and handed it to him.

Brkić said nothing. They shook hands.

Julio spat: He was going, too! He wasn't going to be parted from him!

There wasn't room.

If there were room for one, there was room for two.

It wouldn't hold them.

It would. He'd unhook the heads.

It was dangerous.

Suddenly, I understood everything. This balloon was not going to fly off either into the blue yonder, or to Belgrade, or to Pale. Brkić was afraid. He was afraid of death. He was afraid of solitude. He was afraid of his camp bed and dying at our expense and as a burden to us. It occurred to me that he had in him the spirit of some aging Indian who was preparing for his last journey to the hills. Sometimes I think that life is nothing other than a long, long fear of death.

But Julio gave us the signal. We untied the heads and took them off one by one, then the ropes holding the balloon to the planet. The balloon began to tremble, the board basket to creak. Brkić looked upwards, Julio opened the valve on the other bottle, the one attached to the balloon.

All the ropes were untied. All that could be heard were the flame and the knocking of the taut canvas against the guttering high up in the darkness.

Had Brkić imagined that Julio would let him go alone? They had got through the last war, and they'd get through this one as well. Together. They'd smash fascism into the ground.

And then he began to sing: Arise, despised of the world . . .

The balloon began slowly to rise.

But the bottom of the basket remained, and on it, as on the boards of a little stage, the two of them. Julio watched the balloon, and didn't stop singing. And Brkić held the rope, which was slowly wriggling out of his half-closed fist.

Finally, Julio, too, realized what had happened. He took the rope from Brkić, pulled it, then stopped, knelt down, checked the nails, swore, and then calmed down: What a piece of luck. Had he not got in as well, the basket would have given way somewhere on the journey. His old buddy could have woken up the next day on some fir tree, like a pig on a spit. They ought to have wrapped the rope round the whole basket.

Brkić is ill. He is lying down, pretending to sleep. Julio is beside him, he goes away only to bring him medicines from somewhere. Which Brkić refuses to take.

Davor and Sanja have abandoned their efforts to cheer him up.

When I look up into the sky through the leaves, I see clouds, I feel a cold wind. It seems to me that somewhere behind me a leaf blew away.

This year winter arrived in Sarajevo before autumn. I can't begin to imagine that: the population without water or heating, plastic instead of glass on their windows, tarpaulin instead of roof-tiles. In the rooms icicles, snow, darkness. With no music, no reading, like in caves. That mustn't be allowed to happen. And the baby, in the midst of all that. Diapers, tea, bathing . . . No, it simply couldn't be like that.

Dad, however, asked us to prepare for just that: They won't let us out of the city, we won't let them into the city, we'll go on struggling.

Davor was preparing. He whispered with Sanja, wrote and then burned little notes.

Brkić is lying in the porter's lodge. He's pretending to sleep, because he doesn't want to look, as soon as he opens his eyes, people ask him rubbish, did anything hurt, how was he, did he need anything. Julio no longer went out, except to get medicines, which Brkić wouldn't take. But if he was in the museum, that didn't mean that he was at the patient's bedside. No. He spent most of the day going round the rooms. I know he was looking for Granny's suitcase. He thought that Brkić, on his own or instructing me and Davor, was changing its hiding place. That's why he laid traps. Traces in the dust, objects in special positions, rays which passed through cracks. He set everything up and remembered. I think that mice can no longer have supper without him knowing about it the next day.

That he had seriously intended to find the suitcase and discover what was in it was shown by his sudden interest in macrobiotics, karma, Krishna, and Mother.

So, when we were drinking black tea with Mrs. Flintstone (she had come to return the cigarettes she had borrowed; she had borrowed five and brought back a box), Mother asked her whether she would like milk.

Ugh, over her dead body.

But that's how English people drink it.

That's precisely why she wouldn't. The English are our enemies. The English and the French. Only America and Turkey are neutral. All the others are utral. They were the ones who thought this whole thing up. The Serbs weren't that clever. She wouldn't have tea, either. A little milk on its own, please.

Certainly. I poured some out. I think that as I did so I looked like a cowboy or a Partizan who was having a bullet taken out of a wound. In our family milk is treated like seasoning. It's used to correct the taste of Russian tea, which we have instead of Earl Grey, which we have instead of chicory, which we have instead of coffee, which Julio had exchanged for milk for the pregnant one to drink, and then gave it to a children's home, because Mother said that it was better for the pregnant one to drink seaweed tea.

So, Mrs. Flintstone drank milk without tea, while the three of us drank tea without milk. Our neighbor was desperate. She had come to ask the Doctor to look at a tapestry.

What kind of tapestry?

A yard and a half by two. A frame this thick. Her Junuz had paid one thousand eight hundred marks for it. Original, as though the firm's famous German owner had woven it himself. Julio said that the picture was called *Dressing the Bride*.

Sanja knew that picture. It was by Paja Jovanović.

The bride was wearing Turkish trousers, Mrs. Flintstone was surprised.

Sanja nodded.

But he said it was a Serbian wedding?

In those days in Serbia the Serbs dressed according to Turkish customs.

Really? Could she have a bit more sugar?

Yes, but there wasn't much.

She'd bring us some cubes. Her Junuz had brought some from the front, they'd found it buried behind a Chetnik house. And let them tell her that they hadn't prepared for war. A few days ago they had dug up a gas cylinder as well. Her Junuz brought it by himself. As though their house was a warehouse. Wasn't there someone else who could take things, did her Junuz have to protect every single thing from thieves?

Julio came in. He was carrying two empty jute sacks. He told Mother that, unfortunately, he had only found two. But maybe they wouldn't need more than that.

Mother was embarrassed. None of the three of us knew what he was talking about, which Sanja admitted. But he could hardly wait to explain: Mother had asked for the sacks to plant potatoes in. You rolled back the top of the sack, filled it with earth and then planted seed potatoes in it. When the stalks began to appear, you rolled the top a bit in and added more earth. When the stalks appeared again, you did the same. And you kept watering it. Until the whole sack was filled with earth. Then when the stalks appeared you tied the sack up around them, the potatoes flowered, and after four months you opened the sack and there was no earth in it, only potatoes. American system.

Sanja didn't believe it. Mother was embarrassed. She tried to remember when she had told Julio about this. She had become unsure of herself. For someone who had practiced yoga and eaten seaweed, she was three centuries behind. And that had not happened suddenly. It was happening from one day to the next. She had used up the supplies of grains, miso, umeboshi, kombuo, barley, maltex, and now all she had was flour for *sejtan*. And no one would eat that. Brkić expressed it like this: It's better to go hungry well than to eat badly.

I found her in the cellar, she was chewing a crust of bread and counting little sticks. Those sticks, the stalks of dried yarrow, were a present from Davor. So that she no longer had to throw small coins and apologize to her *I Ching*.

The *I Ching*, or *The Book of Changes*, is one of Mother's holy books, and the only one that is wrapped in silk and kept at a height no less than my own. Mother does not make a single decision or give a single piece of advice without consulting that book. (That's why Brkić refers to that book as the party secretary.) I have read the *I Ching* several times. To start with out of curiosity, then with Mother's encouragement, and finally in order to show off in front of my teacher and schoolmates. Because, for example, to my question whether we ought to leave Sarajevo, one of the answers could be: Carts have wheels, but oxen swish their tails. The leaves of wild pear trees fly south.

Or, to be more precise, when I asked whether I ought to sign up for the civil defense and wash the fighters' socks once a week, I received the answer: Some people use their power where under given circumstances an exalted person refrains from using his. Perseverance now would bring serious consequences, as when a he-goat stumbles into a hedge and his horns become entangled.

The *I Ching* is also known as *The Book of Changes* because it preaches that everything moves and changes, that nothing is without its cause and its consequences. Under its influence, the Serbian poet Crnjanski wrote about pink tracks in the sky. The way the little stalks of yarrow are counted off is connected with our life, and if the message that comes through is properly interpreted, it can help us understand our life better, as well as the powers that shape it and the future into which they may lead us.

However, like all party secretaries, the *I Ching* is not infallible. If its predictions turn out to be wrong, its advice mistaken, its future premature, it is because of our inept, incomplete, and unprofessional interpretation.

That is why the holy book reminds me most of Etienne Suriot's theory about the six dramatic functions and two hundred thousand dramatic situations. (That's the name of his book.) We played that in our literature lessons. The professor would indicate characters by numbers, and then randomly list alongside those numbers several dramatic functions: the hero, the opponent, the wished-for good, the arbiter, the assistant, and the one for whom good was wished. We then translated such schemes into literary plots, usually romances and detective stories. (Need I add who was best at this?)

It was obvious to me that the *I Ching* was a literary form, a novel about which writers dream that they will one day write it, a text out of which incomparably more is read than is written in it.

I asked Mother what was wrong. Why had she gone down to the cellar?

She was afraid.

Of shells?

No. Of the winter. She was afraid for Davor, that he would be taken away. For the baby, that the same thing could happen to them again, in all this chaos. For me, that I'd go blind, writing in the dark. For Dad, that he would be left without a job. She told herself that everyone had his karma, that we were only passing through this life . . . She accepted that, but sometimes she couldn't cope with it. There.

I told her that things would get better, that this war would be over before the winter, that this city had half a million inhabitants . . .
Sometimes our words are like dead birds in an open cage.

Later I saw her laying out Granny's traveling cards. And she looked like Granny. It's strange the way the greatest similarities are revealed in the smallest trifles.

The way someone is sunk in thought, the way he shuffles cards, the way he smiles when he doesn't feel like it, the way he drinks out of a cup, the way he combs his hair, lights a match . . .

A parcel had arrived from Belgrade addressed to Granny, c/o the Jewish Center. Dad brought the news, and Davor or he would go the next day and fetch it. Everyone hoped that it would be in his name, from someone he knew, full of tidbits according to his taste. So Mother hoped that the parcel came from the Belgrade Sai-Center, and that it contained oats, barley, *vibhuti*, the latest collection of poems by Vesna Krmpotić , a life-size picture of Saibaba, yellow rice, and yellow sugar . . . Brkić hoped that the parcel came from his buddies from the Sava, and that it contained plastic bottles of brandy, stuffed in among packs of Drina cigarettes, all interwoven with hot peppers. Sanja was expecting a parcel from her brother, with vitamins and minerals, towels and toothpaste, disposable diapers and a belt for pregnant women. Davor believed that his father was sending him papers for Yugoslav citizenship, and had maybe wrapped in them jars of mayonnaise, olives, and pickled gherkins. I thought that one of my friends who had fled had remembered my love of chocolate, Nescafé, powdered milk, and chocolate. Julio had ordered a packet of scarce medicines, for the nerves and the heart. Only Dad had no desires or expectations. He didn't have anyone in Belgrade.

Today it's a hundred and fifty years since we last had electricity. In the meantime, I've discovered why there is none of this form of energy: (a) because the Chetniks have destroyed the power lines; (b) because the *balijas* (Muslims) don't deliver power so as to stop the Chetniks getting their hands on it as well; (c) because the defenders had removed the oil from the power stations in the city, because it was a kind of gas on which the engines of their Golfs ran; (d) because the miners would not supply the thermoelectric stations with coal because no one was paying for electricity; (e) because the Presidency had decreed that our power should be cut off so that the world would take pity on us; (f) because we sold power to Croatia in exchange for weapons.

I suppose that the truth is somewhere in between. Dismembered.

Without electric energy the pumps can't work, so there's no water. Now it's mostly me who goes to fetch it, sometimes with Dad, sometimes with Davor. He noticed that the police didn't stop people carrying water. We warm the water in the sun, in bottles made of dark glass. It can sometimes be so hot it scalds your hand.

Dad recently pinned to the door ninety-five suggestions for hygienic-epidemiological safety measures. Among other things, because of the lack of water, women, expectant mothers, and children under the age of eighteen—Mother, Sanja, and I—were to use the one toilet with a bowl, while the men should use the other, the so-called squatter. Then the men were ordered, in the name of saving water, to do their big job in newspaper and place it, in the form of a paper ball, in a hole in the garden dedicated to that purpose. To that end, adequate quantities of Granny's newspaper were secured. Of course, we refused this last with disgust and contempt, only Julio was on Dad's side. Since we eat healthy food, for which we have to thank Mother, then our, excuse me, excrement, is fertilizer of great macrobiotic value. It could be packed in little bags, he could already see the advertisement: Halal fertilizer, kosher manure! Natural peat from the seat. Healthy roots in healthy turds!

In order to shut him up, Mother had to promise that she would give serious thought to his proposal.

As often happens in history, the first to infringe the regulations was Martin Luther Dad. Several times, he splashed water after him and then emerged with his newspaper, still engrossed in some article: When did they plan all of this! (That is, the Aggressors.)

A superficial analysis of adherence to Dad's measures would show that the person who stayed longest behind closed doors was Julio. And he always emerged with a damp patch on the back of his overalls. And quarrels weren't rare either. Because of the shortage and saving of water, we had agreed that we could announce our needs, and wherever it was possible to coordinate, two or three needs would be flushed with the same bucket. However, what happened was the reverse. Not only were the actions not announced, nor were the individual results always flushed, with the justification of economy.

I noticed Davor several times coming out of our, the so-called lovelier half's toilet. He was not exposed only because he had been trained earlier to carry out his lesser needs sitting down. Must I say who was the trainer?

Since I have already mentioned her, yesterday the following happened to her: Julio had brought out of the war booty a dress, sleeveless, fastening to halfway down the back, a moderate mini from the wild sixties. Sanja wanted to try it on, and I helped her. When the moment came to take the dress off, complications ensued. First I could hardly undo it because, under pressure of centrifugal forces, the zip had stretched. And then the whole thing got stuck. Partly because of the belly, partly because of cellulite and irritation, the dress stubbornly refused to return to oblivion. The expectant mother in it looked like a sausage with a factory fault.

We were discovered by Davor in this intricate situation. I took a parcel from his hands and he took Sanja from mine. Each of us in the end opened our own.

The parcel had Granny's name on it. It contained neither letter, nor message, nor sign of who was sending it to whom. So we will probably never know who had sent us several pounds of flour and seven rolls of toilet paper.

Davor said that the local police changed the contents of parcels.

Dad thought it was the Chetniks who did it.

And I that life was sometimes very funny.

■ □ ■ □ ■

CHAPTER TWELVE

An example of committed poetry. The Mafia, the Mafia! Davor gets his
mobilization papers. Peanuts. The Prince's unicorn. Things in heaven
. we do not even dream of. Sitting round the tray.

DAVOR CAME BACK WITH FIFTEEN PINTS OF WATER, JUST IN TIME TO
see a clear salt liquid spilling out from under the door of the birdcage. Sanja was crying. What's wrong, asked my brother.

He went in his new trousers.

He hadn't got them dirty.

He had dirtied his gym shoes yesterday. He couldn't keep doing
this. Did he realize that everything had to be washed and cleaned?
He had been pouring oil into the lamps and spilt it! He had been
washing the dishes and left suds on the plates. He had poured tea
and left the strainer clogged. He had played with Sniffy, she was the
one who picked up the hairs. Whatever he did, someone had to follow him and fix things and tidy them. He would be more help to
her if he did nothing. Yes, she was pregnant, but she was not nailed
down. She'd take things slowly, she'd get up early, she'd sleep less,
three hours of sleep were enough for her.

Davor said nothing. He was in the wrong.

Why didn't he say anything? Was she exaggerating again? His
lordship wasn't capable of talking about such banalities as socks,
underpants, crumbs . . .

What crumbs?

Where does he shake the crumbs from the tablecloth?

Into Sniffy's bowl.

That's what he imagined. He shook them out around the bowl as well. Only he chose not to notice. If he noticed, then he'd have to sweep it up. Better let someone else do that. It was easier.

She didn't sweep, did she?

No. His mother swept. She was used to doing it instead of him. Only he no longer lived with his mother. He lived with her.

What had that to do with anything?

Lots. She felt uncomfortable watching her mother-in-law doing it. It wasn't fair.

What wasn't fair?

That his mother was carrying out his tasks in their marriage.

What was so bad about that?

Her eyes were full of tears again: What was bad was that she didn't have a mother.

And then she bit her lip and fell silent. She was making an effort not to cry, but somehow her tears always let her down. It was five years since that death, but the pain remained. If it hadn't increased, it hadn't got any less either.

Maybe that was why Davor said nothing and risked waking up one day covered in hen-peckings. He'd like to take Sniffy out for a walk, the storm would subside, but it was still daylight. He wouldn't want to meet Mrs. Flintstone at this time of day. Knowing her, it would happen to her quite by chance.

However, she, Mrs. Flintstone, appeared of her own accord. This time with her head packed in a scarf, the immobilization of a fracture of the jaw model. That scarf is called a *shamia*, and for women, in this latest awakening of national consciousness, it has the same magical power as a green beret for men or a navy-blue-black French cap for pensioners.

She flew in on the wings of a leaflet—I don't know who gave it to her, but I can guess. The leaflet said, I paraphrase: freedom, honor, aggression, pride, freedom, blood, defense, aggression, homeland, families, independent, sovereign, indivisible, donorship! Every family should make a gift of gold or hard currency to the Defense Forces. The wealthiest families should give fifty grams, and socially disadvantaged families one gram. Or the equivalent in German marks.

Mother accepted the leaflet. She was expected to fill in how well off our family was. Mrs. Flintstone informed us that everyone was giving rings, bracelets, gold chains. No one had yet filled in the slot for people on benefits, social cases.

Mother couldn't do it without Dad.

Then the activist would return later. She was going to visit everyone else in the street. She stopped, came back and gave Mother another piece of paper. Her Rambo had written a poem, and I should see whether anything needed correcting and then Davor could take it to the Radio. (Rambo was a daughter!) I can't resist reproducing it in full:

> *My Mother removed her gold wedding ring*
> *To defend the town from a christening.*
> *My Uncle took out all his teeth of gold*
> *To drive the Chetniks away from our fold.*
> *My Auntie took off her most precious chain*
> *To buy more bullets for our just campaign.*
> *My Granny's carrying a real old ducat*
> *So the Chetniks will all kick the bucket.*
> *And in front of them all walks my proud Dad*
> *Carrying the gold pistol that made him glad.*
> *Come one and all, bring whatever you can*
> *To drive the Chetniks out to their last man!*

My teacher would have had things to say about the rhythm and meter, and the language wasn't exactly anything to write home about either, at least not according to the rules we had learned. But the poem was sincere. Committed verse. Yesterday it was Tito and the Krauts, today it's a Bosnian uncle and the Chetniks. Yesterday a red five-pointed star, today a gold fleur-de-lis.

That same afternoon, Mother acquainted Dad with the questionnaire. Dad read it and tore it up without a word. *Placet!* Then he sat down and gave a deep, deep sigh. Mother had taught him that yoga trick, but this time it didn't help.

Dad was losing the ground under his feet: He didn't think he was going to manage to defend the museum. And then nothing else made any sense. It was like underground water. First you feel damp and cold, and then the walls collapse. This was not his Bosnia. (I knew what he meant: the head scarves, the greetings in the language of the desert, the songs sung more through the nose than the mouth, the soldiers with bandanas round their heads like Ninja Turtles.) Little by little, people were leaving the city. Without saying goodbye. And whoever left was not thinking of coming back.

Mother looked at him: Whatever Bosnia was like, God made it as it is and everything that was happening here now was according to His will.

Mother says this like the most natural thing in the world. That's what she thinks. Faith is like drunkenness that numbs the nerves, so you neither feel pain, nor recognize fear. And like all other anesthetics, they achieve the best results when they pierce and frighten someone else. For Dad, however, God exists far more as a fundamental political and historical fact, whom it is not possible to ignore, and far less as the God in whom his family had believed and who even now, through the eyes of his mother, watched him thoughtfully from every recollection of his childhood.

Dad talked to a colleague from the Jewish community. They organized convoys for evacuating their members from Sarajevo. Even Davor could get out.

Could Davor and Sanja (and I) go, and Mother stay with him?

No. Mother was the only authentic Jew. She could take them with her, but not send them instead of her.

After she had placed her questionnaires with one eye and ear, while taking care with the others that the Doctor should not escape, Mrs. Flintstone clattered over in her slippers, giving Mother just enough time for the slow digestion of what Dad had proposed to her.

Mrs. Flintstone had done up her woolen waistcoat and firmly tied her woolen scarf round her back, so she looked both blown up and trussed at the same time: Had the honored Doctor of historical sciences read the advertisement?

Yes.

She had wanted him to fill it in, but she didn't want to take up his time. The Doctor certainly had more urgent business. But on the other hand, nothing was more important than the struggle. These lovely mountains round Sarajevo had to be cleaned up.

Dad interrupted impatiently: What exactly did she want? And without waiting for an answer, he handed her the two halves of the torn-up leaflet.

She was confused. She wanted to ask what had happened, but didn't know how. Kindly? Sternly? With understanding? The words were probably already beginning to chirrup in her consciousness that tearing up a state leaflet was like tearing up the state. All that went on in silence behind her wide-open mouth, so Dad continued: She should tell the gentlemen who had signed it that he was not in a position to fulfill their expectations.

Had the doctor torn it up . . .

Yes. And read it! And seen the seal, and the signatures. There was no category for his family. We were not a social case. We were just an unfortunate one. We had no German marks, we had no home, we had no work, we had no jewelry, we had no gold. We had nothing! We were paupers! (That's what Dad called himself and all the other stunted descendants of once powerful and wealthy families. Preserving their honor rather than power, honesty rather than justice, beauty rather than wealth, with time those families had declined and vanished, like stone signposts fallen into weeds, earth, and oblivion. Their large house made of clay bricks, almost a century and a half old, had been sold and demolished. I remember vaguely, as though from a dream. In its place there was now a concrete cube. A garage had obliterated the lilacs, asphalt had been poured over the cobblestones in the courtyard, the greasy-black iron pipe on the fountain had been replaced by a nickel tap. Had she not died before all that, Gran, Dad's Mother, would have died of shame and surprise, unhappy to see her children climbing onto the devil's stuck out tongue as though it were Allah's golden road. Dad was the only one of her children not to have begun to speak her language, and he was the only one she understood. He was the only one who did not believe, and the only one whom she believed.)

Mrs. Flintstone was fitting the two halves of her unfortunate leaflet together as though they were a puzzle of eighty pieces. She turned them round, turned them over, leaned one against the other: You mean nothing at all!

Nothing!

Everyone else had contributed.

We're not contributing.

We could borrow something. She'd ask her Junuz.

Thank you, there's no need.

She had seen with her own eyes one old dear take the ring from her finger. With a stone This size. Ducats . . . gold chains . . . pendants . . .

Dad had partly accompanied her and partly pushed her out. When he came back, he was red, the two lines on his forehead looked like lightning. He was a fool for forgetting himself in front of her. A confounded idiot! He would have liked most to have shoved all those papers up her nose. The Mafia would try anything! Tomorrow the whole town would be trumpeting that the Director of the museum was a Chetnik. He would not allow the sommies to move into the museum, he would not allow any of the gold to leave the treasury, he would not allow any of the weapons to be taken from the collection, he would not give paintings for auction. He was hiding his son from mobilization, he was not responding to donorship . . .

Davor wasn't his son.

Those were subtleties for the *mahala*. They would make this city into the biggest *mahala* in the world. The Mafia. The Mafia! (This is not the title of a musical about Sarajevo. When Dad says Mafia, he doesn't mean criminals, drugs, gambling, prostitution. Dad is a historian. For him the Mafia is one of the autochthonous forms of military organization: the Mafia is a historically verified movement. It is an absolutely well-known way to transfer democratic rights and liberty from the individual, as consumer, onto the family. You have to read Machiavelli. It's all there. He proved scientifically and pre-determined the direction history would go. He, and not *I Ching*s or whisky and cards. What's this game called . . . This is a war of families, and that is why the old expressions, names, and customs are surfacing now, that is why belief is once again meddling and thrusting itself into affairs of state.)

(Dad's favorite film is *The Godfather*.)

As we had quite rightly feared, this wasn't the end of it. Not even two days had gone by, when, in the porter's lodge, I was handed call-up papers for Davor. Davor was to report to the local council office, to be allocated to a unit. Mobilization.

As I had been previously advised, I didn't want to sign the paper. But the young man was kind, he signed for me. Davor yelled at me later because of that. Why had I talked to him at all, why had I taken the paper, why had I let the courier into the museum!

Mother mentioned the convoy. She would do everything she could to protect him. Even if it meant leaving Sarajevo. All they had to do was tell Dad whether they wanted to go.

Davor did. He didn't want to join any kind of army. He didn't want to kill anyone.

Sanja said nothing. What did she think about this: That it was good and sensible. He had to get out of here. Unfortunately, she couldn't.

There'd be a doctor on the convoy.

She hadn't gone by plane, and she wouldn't be going by bus, either. She had stayed to take care of her pregnancy and she didn't want to risk anything. And she didn't believe that the Serbs would allow Davor to pass just like that.

Mother wasn't going to try to persuade her. Let her stay. But Davor had to be taken care of, too. (Everyone thinks of their own baby. And as for the other side, Dad was sure it was safe.)

Davor wasn't going without Sanja.

He must be sensible! Who knows whether he'd ever have another chance of getting out of Sarajevo. She'd follow him as soon as the baby was born.

No! He wasn't going without Sanja.

But what about the call-up papers? His mobilization?

What about them? He wouldn't go.

They'd come for him.

He'd say he worked at the Radio.

But they already knew that Davor didn't work there anymore. They also knew that he had already been in the army, and that because of his sight he was excused certain duties, such as keeping watch, they knew that he was hiding in the museum and that his wife was pregnant. It was Junuz who told us everything they knew about him.

Junuz would now come three times in the course of a day, to visit the museum and specifically Brkić. Sometimes he brought him cigarettes, sometimes tobacco, but always a bottle as well, pocket size. They met like men, and got drunk like pigs. Today, exceptionally, Junuz had brought a jar of pork cracklings, to rub on his joints. There was no bird like a little pig, it flew low and was easily caught. When Junuz's children asked what they were eating, Julio said peanuts. They wanted to try them, and Junuz gave them some. Brkić watched the saucer empty. The children evidently liked peanuts.

Junuz smoked more than Brkić. He lit cigarettes with a Zippo lighter, which lit in the wind and under water. When his cigarette had burned halfway down, the smoke rose up through his mustache. His walkie-talkie, or as it is now called his Motorola, was kept in the top pocket of his overall. It kept tickling him under the chin with its antenna, and he chased it away as though mosquitoes were attacking him.

Davor's problem is solved, for the time being. He's on the list of Junuz's fighters. With Julio. I think this was thanks mainly to Brkić, but also to the strangest man in this museum, my Dad. Junuz's unit was to move into one wing of the museum and they would have the right to use the counter of the old Jewish apothecary's as a bar. The duties of the good soldier Schweik were reduced to guarding the checkpoint in one of the neighboring streets. In return he would get accreditation and be able to move freely about town.

So, Davor kept watch. By his own admission, what he did was doze for two hours in the course of the night in an armchair surrounded by sacks with coffee written on them and in which there was sand, holding on to his rifle the whole time, so as not to slide off the chair in his sleep. For those two hours Sanja's care and love watched over him.

She woke up at the same time as him, in the middle of the night, wrapped herself in Sniffy and blankets, lit the lamp, using up oil, read, and waited. When the warrior returned to the birdcage, there was a kiss and a warm bed awaiting him. The timetable of his shifts was recorded in her notebook, along with details of the regularity and quality of her stools. When he got up, he had warmed clothes waiting for him, and when he returned, hot tea in a thermos. He found everything he thought he had forgotten in his pocket, when he had quite given up hope: scarf, hat, gloves. And in another pocket, what she had put aside from her maternity income: a piece of pie, a sweet, a square of chocolate.

The baby whose aunt I shall be was very restless. I was put in the stupid position of kneeling on the floor with my ear on someone else's stomach. It was worth it. I heard something like a gallop, and imagined a little naked boy emerging from a lake on a unicorn. As the birth drew nearer, Sanja was increasingly calm and confident, and I ever nearer the edge of panic: The hospital was destroyed, there were no medicines, hygiene was on the verge of heavy metal. They didn't know a doctor whom they could pay to make everything all right, nor did they have the money to pay such a doctor.

At Brkić's request, Junuz had prepared a car especially for Sanja. But what if that day there was some particularly fierce shelling. What if before then the fuel was stolen from the car? It's true that it was under guard, but someone told me that guards sleep.

If people don't talk about something, that doesn't mean they're not thinking about it. If they don't mention someone, it doesn't mean they have forgotten him. Whenever I see the two of them holding hands and looking at each other's empty laps, I remember what they've already gone through.

Perhaps she was taking care of them now?

Perhaps.

She was an angel. All babies who die become angels. She had read about that. She would watch over her little sister as well.

How did she know it was a little sister?

That's just how it seemed to her.

And what would she prefer?

A little girl. What about him?

He didn't care. As long as everything was all right.

Davor kept watch at a crossroads. He sat beside a barrier. The barrier was down, but at such a level that cars could pass underneath it, without the guard having to get up. But people had to bend down. The asphalt at that crossroads, as in most of the city, was pitted with the traces of explosions. Shallow round holes in the asphalt, with ray-like scars in the direction from which the shell came remind one of the traces of giant birds. Harpies, perhaps? (People travel and write travelogues. I have stayed and I'm writing a stayologue about it all.)

Brkić seems to be a little better. But he won't hear of going to hospital. Because of him, Mother has reemerged from her underground world. She is our Persephone. The goddess of grains, who brings springtime with her arrivals and with her departures autumn.

The patient eats oats, wheat, barley, rice, and bran. He drinks salt teas with the scent and taste of the sea, and his general improvement is attributed to Mother. We all gather round him, in the porter's lodge. Shells continue to pound the surrounding hills every day but now that has acquired the rhythm of something customary. Like the sound of a cockcrow at dawn, for instance.

The smokers roll cigarettes. There are special little machines for that ritual, but Brkić doesn't see the soul in that. They use paper which Dad gave them, so-called flimsy, on which the minutes of meetings of the activist communist workers of the museum used to be typed out. I came across Brkić several times reading the cigarette which was burning up between his fingers. Opium for the people was being transformed into smoke and ash. The cigarettes stank, because they were half-filled with a mixture of tobacco from stubs, and half with crumbled lime or coltsfoot for tea. Junuz brought real cigarettes, Julio did as well, but Dad exchanged them at the market for food, depriving horses of it. He went into town several times a day, to supervise the evacuation of exhibits to a more secure location, in keeping with the law. That gave him the opportunity to have supreme command of prices and relations at the market, and in that, in my humble opinion, he surpassed Julio.

Dad says that for modern man shopping is like hunting in prehistory. Regardless of whether he was buying rice, tapestries, or books, the contemporary hunter revived atrophied instincts of strength, speed, and power, in sensual pleasure of unlimited possession. The longer this war lasts, the more books that he read long ago open up in Dad like flowers, and he's less and less a doctor of dry Latin phrases and more and more a wise man whose words fly off down the wind like blossom petals.

If a stranger were to come now, say from Belgrade, he would surely be surprised as to why all the cups, so called *fildžans,* stand crookedly —leaning over. (The reader notices that the description of the ritual of drinking coffee—coffeeing—imposes on the writer the obligation to correct the language he uses.) The containers are crooked in order for the dregs (sediment) to drain better. Unlike the prewar *džezvas,* the wartime ones are clean inside. The person on duty, before pouring, washes (sweeps) the walls with a teaspoon, which increases the quantity of cream (foam), which is then shared out again with a teaspoon equally among all the *fildžans.* This sitting around a tray (salver) with the coffee on it, or rather the surrogate for coffee, is essential for another reason as well. It takes the place of news. In the course of the day, everyone hears something, wherever he happens to be and from his own sources, and then those discoveries are united into something, which, if it were composed in lines, would be epic poetry. (This is one example of a stayologue.)

Julio had heard that it was possible to get out of Sarajevo with the help of Unprofor. By plane.
Everyone had heard that.
And would it be possible for Mother's son?
Yes.
With Sanja?
He wasn't sure. You had to pay a certain sum, and get a certain PRESS card. You arranged for some foreign agency to take him on as their correspondent, and then they invited him and he got on the plane, and bye.
Sanja liked the idea. Davor would be able to go like that, and she would follow him later.
It was out of the question that he should go and leave his pregnant wife in this shit. (Instead of Sarajevo, people more and more often referred to this shit, this hell, this chaos, this madness.)
Brkić thought it was out of the question as well.

■ □ ■ □ ■

CHAPTER THIRTEEN

A short course in biorhythmic nutrition. In one hand a pencil, in the other crossed fingers. What Sanja leaves under her pillow for me. The blue smoke of damp pine wood. An intruder in the women's cubicle. Spiritual levels and arrogance. The craziest night so far.

SOMEONE KICKED THE DOOR. DAVOR LEAPT UP TO HIDE, AND THEN remembered that he had accreditation, and sat down again. Dad went to open the door. He came back with none other than Mrs. Flintstone. She had knocked with her foot because she was carrying a tray with real coffee on it. In other words, without additional roast chicory, roast lentils, roast bran, roast barley.

Why, I wondered to myself. The question was apt, because there are people who won't do anything without some reason or purpose, and particularly not something of use to or for the pleasure of others. Roughly like when Sniffy lies on his back. He sticks all four legs in the air and allows us to scratch his tummy. After that he gets a piece of dried crust.

Mrs. Flintstone had come for us to make peace, although she had not forgiven either Dad, or Julio, or Brkić. There was great interest in us in the *mahala*, however, and she could discover exclusive news at its source: Her Junuz had said that Brkić was ill, while here he was glowing with health.

Brkić said nothing, but continued cutting a match lengthwise in two with a razor blade, making two matches out of one.

And Mrs. Flintstone had nearly brought one *fildžan* less. She thought she wouldn't find him alive. (First reason: She had come to see whether we could soon hope for some grieving.)

Macrobiotics, said Julio, and continued to praise Mother and her healing skills. Real coffee was being drunk, and there had to be some conversation. Dad backed Julio up: Mother had cured several people of cancer. He remembered also how she had cured people of obesity, kidney stones, ulcers . . .

Mrs. Flintstone had no reason not to believe the Doctor, even if Julio, with his children's lunch packets, sex chakras, and thermometer had gambled away her confidence in him: What did the Director's lady use for her cures? Herbs?

No. Food.

More precisely, correct nutrition. Grains, seaweed, pulses . . . Dad had begun to lose his hair and Mother had put a stop to that. He couldn't take algae in his food, so she added it secretly.

Julio thought that Mother used grasses for her treatments. Algae were grasses only in the sea.

Dad pointed to Brkić. He was an obvious success of Mother's.

Julio also knew of some cases of cures. He had a friend who had one arm shorter than the other. He ate sponges and crushed coral and in a month his arm had grown. But it grew longer than the healthy one. In New Zealand they had banned people from eating coral. They had devoured two of their islands. Abroad, every hotel with five stars and a crescent had to have a Swedish table just for biorhythmic guests.

Dad laughed. He said that Julio was making things up as usual.

Davor remembered that he had had a problem with his stools and Mother's grain cakes had helped. The most important thing in them was the bran. (Mrs. Flintstone was on the point of believing, but then hesitated. She had heard of people eating grains, but you fed bran to livestock.)

Mother listed the grains: barley, millet, oats . . .

Julio said that he had eaten oats in the last year, and that he had great difficulty in stopping neighing.

Brkić didn't think that was because of the oats.

What then?

Something hereditary.

Mother saw that the times were propitious, the wind was blowing into her sails, and she began one of her litanies against meat in the diet. After that those who listened to her were ashamed that they had livers, rumps, and drumsticks of their own. When she came to the place where people's unpleasant smells came from meat they had eaten decaying in their intestines, the question flew out in front of her: What was it, for example, for instance, that made a *hinsan* man's feet stink?

Eating protein of animal origin.

Meat?

Meat, eggs, milk. But primarily meat.

It wasn't from sweating then, or because they didn't wash?

Sweating only threw out onto the surface gases that formed from decaying carrion one had eaten.

But her Junuz didn't eat, God forbid, carrion.

What did he eat?

Freshly slaughtered meat, pink, baked under a lid . . .

As soon as it was slaughtered, it was dead. And every dead body was a corpse.

But you couldn't cook a living animal. It's humane . . .

It's a matter of not cooking an animal at all.

You mean potatoes with nothing?

You needn't eat potatoes either.

Oh! Mrs. Flintstone was beginning to wriggle: All right, so what did Mother put under the lid of her pot?

Pita. Bread. Rolls . . .

And what for instance as an example, was she to cook so that her Junuz's feet weren't onerous. Did Mother have some suitable bio-rhythmic recipes?

She should try combinations. Lentils, rice, soya flour, algae . . . Mother would give her a little seaweed, if she wanted to try.

Yes, she would.

Mrs. Flintstone could be accused of all sorts of things, but the courage and curiosity of a Columbus were certainly not what she lacked. She came with coffee, and she left with seaweed. At the formal send-off, Julio said that you could use sponge instead of seaweed, only it had to be natural.

Mrs. Flintstone said she knew that.

Julio wasn't sure what would happen next. Would the newly baked macrobiotic fan put the seaweed into rice or would she make her Junuz rub his feet with it.

Fata had forgotten something so she came back. She kept meaning to ask, her children had eaten some kind of peanuts with Brkić. She roasted them, salted them, shelled them, didn't shell them, peeled them, didn't peel them, no good. They weren't like Uncle Brkić's. And she wanted to ask where you could buy those ones?

Mother didn't know anything about it, while Julio had to go out in a hurry.

When Davor appeared in the park this morning, the color of his face was chalk white. Fata called that color *tabut*-color. (A *tabut* is a yellow pine board on which a dead person wrapped in a white shroud is carried and buried.) I was picking dandelion roots, while Sanja was sitting on a bench and fabricating vitamin D under the influence of the sun's rays.

Davor sat down on the bench beside her. She put her arms round him and he toppled onto her lap. Pietà. It was obvious that someone had pulled all the larger bones out of my brother's body. And that after several days when he had just begun to resemble himself, an old warrior and knight.

He was desperate: Today he had to take the oath. And sign it. That he would fight for Bosnia and Herzegovina. (As he had previously signed, as the majority of others had done, before the war, that he would also fight for Yugoslavia.) He couldn't do it. He didn't know what to do.

Let him go with Sanja to the doctor's today. It was quiet, they could go slowly. That would be his justification for today. And they'd think of something for tomorrow.

What?

That he was pregnant as well! They'd think of something. They'd set off on foot, then hitch a lift. When people saw her with her stomach, they'd stop for sure.

I was amazed. When bean stew had to be made, she had problems if it hadn't been arranged in advance. And now suddenly, she was going out of the museum, after almost two months, with no arrangement, preparation, or plan. Mother pressed a little sandalwood powder onto her forehead.

———

When they had gone, Brkić and Julio cleaned their room. Brkić dusted, while Julio moved the larger pieces of furniture and cleaned behind and underneath them. As he did so he looked for, but didn't find, Granny's little suitcase. This was the last room he had not scrutinized. For a few moments he sat, spiritually broken, like the captain of a burning yacht, while the current carried him toward an island where his salvation lay. (See the story "McCoy's Seed" by Jack London. That's another of the books which Sanja puts under my pillow from time to time. I read them as though I were dreaming. Where does she find them! Sometimes I'm ashamed in the face of this talent of hers. Out of a pile of rags on a fair stall, she would draw a black athletic top for the baby! In a supermarket in a provincial suburb, she would shake the dust off boxes containing Italian shoes. She, like no one else I know, particularly not my teacher or Davor, was able to approach kitsch, an abyss, or a fiery furnace, and return, bearing in her arms a real, genuine, simple piece of art, snatched from destruction or fire. That was talent. She didn't write, paint, or play an instrument, but, of this I'm certain, she often blew more life into a work than its writer did. That was the secret of her connivance with kitsch. My teacher had recommended Salinger's *Catcher in the Rye* to us, while she favored his stories. Davor listened to Okudzhava singing, while Sanja brought along *Travels of a Dilettante*. The whole of that winter I signed my letters, notes, and messages with the name "Mr. Schonhoven." And let me not list all the films she had given me tickets for.)

The lime tree is still green, but dusk catches up with us with jobs unfinished. The gutters are blocked with fallen leaves. The wind beats on broken doors. Pensioners go out in caps and coats, windows are left shut during the day, the bottles of dark glass in which water was heated in the sun have disappeared from windowsills together with pots of flowers. The carts that carry canisters of water in the afternoon are loaded with wood in the morning. Chimneys puff out the thick, blue smoke of fresh pine wood. The hills in the pine forests are bald. Where there were cemeteries covered in weeds and trees, bare ground now stretches overnight. Out of the tall grass only stumps and headstones peer, equally high and bright against the dark background. Together with rain, mists now fall over the city. When we breathe, visible steam comes out of our mouths. Those who take Sniffy out early for walks tread on fallen green quinces and walnuts.

In our lives the war has taken on the place of a domesticated stray dog or a mangy kitten found on a garbage dump. It likes being with us, it feeds on what we have left over or what it steals from us. Politicians, leaders, and führers pretend to go to meetings and negotiations, and we pray and live for the moment when one of us will take the earphones of the Walkman off his ears and say: The war is over! Dear listeners, as of this morning there is peace.

We are the listeners, the ordinary people. Even when there are no batteries and no power, even when the lines are cut and when the radio receivers and antennae are broken, and when, in cellars, in the dark, we listen only to detonations and muffled weeping, we are dear listeners. They comfort us that we are the people, that we are citizens, that all of this is for our sake and in our interest. It's no more than we deserve since we had got used to living between the television set and our cars. Dear listeners, the Aggressor has renewed his attacks. Dear listeners, the enemy has provoked us. Dear listeners, civilians have died again . . . Dear listeners, as of this morning there is still war. And it will never stop! Every shell that has fallen, every bullet fired, every piece of shrapnel and grenade, all that is seed. This war will not even be over, and another one will spring up. Dear sheep droppings, stop waiting for peace. As of this morning, your life is war. Find your place in it. The sooner, the better.

(I've really sentimentalized this sentimentally. But I'm so tired that I don't have the strength to tear up this page.)

So, yesterday was yesterday. Davor and Sanja went for a checkup. During their absence Julio made one more unsuccessful attempt at finding Granny's suitcase. But I have already noted that. In a pause in his search he broke the toilet bowl in our women's cubicle. I was the first to hear the crashing and banging, and when I reached the scene of the accident Julio was just completing pulling on his overall. On the concrete, the lid sticking out, swayed the broken bowl.

This was how it was revealed quite by chance not only that Julio used the women's cubicle but that he did not sit on the seat, but squatted. He is still very ashamed because of all this, and he's not asking Brkić and Davor what it would cost to mend the damage.

Commander Junuz came to ask Davor why he had not been at the formal oath-taking ceremony. When he described what it had all looked like, the first thing that occurred to me was the ceremony of my joining the Young Pioneers. Flags, scarves, harmonica, singing and chanting in unison, applause on one's own account. And since the response had been enormous, and there was a big crowd, the fighters had not signed up then and there, they'd do it tomorrow—today—in the headquarters. And Davor must be sure to come, because some people are already wondering what happened to him.

Good morning, this above us is the sky, it can sometimes be, when it is a clear day, et cetera. I sang and whistled the whole day. And when I asked myself why, I could find no other reason than the fact that the ultrasound had shown that everything was fine with Sanja and the little horseman. According to the calculations of the orbits of the moon, the stars, and the suns, the future scorpion had kicked and tumbled its way into the ninth month.

Now, when it seemed that everything was all right with Sanja, Davor was able to abandon himself completely to self-pity. He had to sign an obligation that he would defend a state he did not care about and in which he was not thinking of staying. Julio consoled him: the hand wrote, the heart erased. In one hand a pencil, in the other crossed fingers. It was better to be a *mujahadin* than a *janissary*.

Dad had been at one of the fateful meetings about the destiny of the museum, at my request Mother measured the spiritual level and arrogance of the lodgers present. (She did this by spinning a plumb line over a clock, reading in its movement the general course of forces in the universe. Our spiritual level was a positive omen, and it indicated the degree to which our soul, traveling through various bodies and lives, had come on its journey to God. Our arrogance was a negative omen, it indicated the quantity of stubbornness with which we rejected the idea of the immortality of the soul and mocked yarrow, Sai-Bur Hendrix, and Hare Krishna. In short, arrogance was an inclination to materialism and cynicism. Mother's plumb line could have come in useful to McCarthy in his hunt for communists, because it disclosed me and Brkić infallibly. We were the only ones to have a degree of arrogance higher than our spiritual level. The highest spiritual level, ten, was Mother's.)

When the plumb line stopped spinning, Sanja gave herself up to depilation (in the vernacular: dehairification, defuzzation?), while Julio, after unsuccessful attempts at consoling him, withdrew into Brkić's chambers. I was thus left to put my shoulders under the heavenly vault of Davor's fears and anxieties: He wouldn't be able to do it. This war had nothing to do with him. If he had wanted to fight, he would have gone off to the army to which he had already sworn allegiance and in which he had served. He was not a fighter, he was a producer. What kind of fighter was he, when he didn't even know how to dismantle a rifle? And who was he to shoot? His father, perhaps?

I reminded him of a scene from the novel *The Bridge Over The Drina,* when the hero, Alihodza, his ear nailed to the wooden gate of the bridge, refuses to accept the help of an Austrian soldier, because all he can see, through his tears of pain and the blood from his wound, is the red cross on the soldier's sleeve. Was my brother also beginning to see the people around him through blood and tears? Figurative, incidentally.

Since I have mentioned ears, I know that one of his friends, a musician, at the beginning of the war, went around cutting off the ears of dead Yugoslav army soldiers. His friend. Cutting off ears.

Our neighbors took care of us . . .

Did I know what *kurban* was?

Yes. Meat.

A ram. A sacrifice. It's bought and fed. Children are allowed to play with it. They come to love it. They give it a name. Then for Bairam the grown-ups cut its throat. Those neighbors I'm talking about, that's those children, who don't know what tomorrow will bring, and they don't know why things are like they are today. Our neighbors will weep for their lambkins. But who asks the neighbors?

If I had read this somewhere, it would never have crossed my mind that these were my brother's words. He, who talked about art,

Hitchcock, nature, music, training dogs, directing, was now talking about the Turks, slaughter, impaling, and cutting off ears. All afternoon, I stared out of the window, as though poisoned, paralyzed, sickened. That murky and tangled past was now coming out of people in stinking boils and the stench from it covered everything within my field of vision enclosed by hills, fog, and smoke.

Brkić had learned another favorite word: rump. And a few evenings ago he had said to Junuz: Every town in Bosnia was its own rump. And Junuz asked him what was Serbia then, since it was sticking its nose into each of them?

I couldn't help Davor. Bent under his sky, he went off dragging his feet. He came back two hours later, aghast. He had been at the headquarters. Waited. Some secretary wasn't there, and she hadn't come. The list to be signed was with her. Locked in her desk. Davor hadn't signed anything. He had only signed for equipment. Short trousers, two left boots. He should wait till they heard from the man who'd taken two right ones.

Davor had to admit, first to himself and then to everyone he had splashed with his hogwash mood, that the whole ceremony of signing a formal obligation had not been organized only because of him, with the aim of morally shaking one young Serbian intellectual and breaking him as a person. Although there was still reason for anxiety, locked in some drawer, the rubber doll called Davor had been reinflated and for a time it would appear as though he had a spine. Brkić, as usual, said this more briefly and accurately: The brave die once, cowards a hundred times.

Thus was the steel tempered.

At two o'clock Mother announced the arrival of the team to pour oil into the substation. I was walking with Sniffy and confirmed the news. At seven o'clock, we were sitting looking at the light bulb. At half-past seven we had given up hope that it would light up. At eight o'clock we discovered that our neighbors had power. At two minutes past eight we established that our light was not broken, the cooker was switched on, the washing machine and television likewise. At nine o'clock we were getting ready for bed. At nine-thirty Granny opened the fridge and squeaked. Or else the fridge squeaked.

Anyway, there was a light inside. Perhaps we would not have known, had not Sniffy popped up beside Granny and started wagging his tail. It is incredible that he can jump from the deepest sleep even at the slightest sound that has any connection with food: opening the fridge, sticking a knife into a tin, collecting crumbs with the hand. Granny can't stand him only because he catches her in every theft.

Sniffy's tail knocked over a vase of ikebana and that marked the beginning of one of the craziest nights in the course of the war up to now. We all stood up, not understanding how the light in the fridge could be on, while the lamps, radio, television and cooker stayed cold. Davor checked the connections, everything was in order. Dad went for Junuz, they checked the substation and they established that two so-called phases were not switched on.

Sanja plugged in the vacuum cleaner, but Davor hurried to take her place. Mother jumped out of bed into a cloud of flour. Sanja then separated the washing and filled the machine with one heap, and a pot on the cooker with the other. I broke two eggs and together with oil and the blender I hurried to mix mayonnaise. Julio decided to grind some coffee surrogate. Dad checked the blackout, fixing the blinds where necessary. And then the power went off. A few tears dropped into the mixture in the blender. Julio transferred the little pieces of chicory into the hand mill. Mother added more flour, salt, and cold water. Davor lit candles so as to finish the cleaning with a broom. The washing in the machine stopped gurgling and continued smelling. Brkić stopped cursing the television, and continued cursing the power. He doesn't normally look at the speaking box, but does so because of Granny, who needs subtitles even during the breaks. It seems that those responsible heard him, because the power came back.

Mother added a bit more flour, sugar, and tepid water. Davor went to pour softener into the machine, so that Sanja wouldn't catch cold. Sanja remembered that she could complete the electrical depilation of her bikini-zone. Julio transferred the chicory to the electric grinder. When he had finished, he borrowed Dad's electric razor. Dad switched on the nickel-cadmium battery charger, and then went down to the cellar to use the electric saw to cut chipboard planks into pieces the size of our little stove. Sanja remembered a machine called the peace-maker, for pressure steam-cleaning. Her knight, of course, couldn't allow that. He took the spear with a brush on the top and attacked the tiles. Mother's bread started to rise, the beans in the first water had come to the boil, my mayonnaise had started to look like the commercial kind.

The image on the television danced in the rhythm of the movements of my blender, and not in the rhythm of the song which some people on the screen were singing in some ruins or other. Although I couldn't hear them, I knew that they were singing, because they were swaying to left and right, and their mouths were constantly open. Then the song was replaced by the news. Brkić changed channels. There people were singing again, swaying with open mouths, only in the background, instead of ruins, there was a tricolor, with the Serbs' four hooked S letters.

That song was replaced by the news as well. Brkić and Granny were dozing. The picture on the screen showed some hill, from where a young man was aiming with his finger at the scorched city. The camera came closer and, among other houses and buildings, I could see our museum, and people, like ants in an anthill, like beetles in a potato field, like snails in a cabbage patch. Luckily, the power went off again. We all stayed where we were and waited. Then Mother took the bread out to get cool. Sanja cried. Davor consoled her: Had she taken the depilator (hairplucker, defuzzer) straight away and not got the peace-maker out, she would have finished. Besides, even if there was no power, one had to shave. Dad came back from the substation. Our fuses had blown. Because of the phases. Junuz again. The substation again. Operation connecting phases. We had power again.

The bread was baked. The beans hissed. The little hairs sizzled. The mayonnaise thickened. The depths of night.

We are all on edge, tired, angry, and we are not happy. As though we had stolen something. Without power, we do things slowly, we discuss things, plan things, gather round the sunlight and round the fire. When the light bulb comes on, like tonight, the good household ghosts scuttle away from us into the corners like mice. It seems that many things are seen better in the dark.

So then why do we still wait so greedily for every new announcement of power. It's as though, without ourselves knowing it yet, we are all pieces of electrical equipment.

(I wrote this part earlier, by mistake, on the other side of the note-book. And when it appeared here, I wanted to tear out the pages and stick them where they belonged. But then I decided against it. Maybe it's even better for them to stay here. This isn't a diary in any case.)

■ □ ■ □ ■

CHAPTER FOURTEEN

Deblockade of the city. Davor and Brkić leave. *Domini canes.* Instructions for Sniffy-management. Good night, Leader. The secret of Granny's suitcase.

LAST NIGHT DAVOR DIDN'T COME HOME AFTER HIS SHIFT. SANJA anxiously asked whether we knew what had happened to him. We remembered that Julio could go and check up. But Julio wasn't there either. Sanja then offered to take my place in the porter's lodge, and I went to bed. As usual, I didn't remember what I dreamed, and I deliberately missed that part of the morning ritual. I dropped into the coffee ceremony just in time to learn that Sanja had been replaced on watch by Dad who had then gone first thing in the morning to Davor's headquarters. All his questions had been answered by a shrug of the shoulders. Mother didn't show any signs of panic, although the stories seeping through the town were beginning to worm-eat her as well. This revolution, like all revolutions incidentally, devoured other people's children.

I don't know whether it was because he was wiry or bony, but it didn't devour Davor. He came home just before lunch. We learned that they had all been in a state of military alert. He and his group had sat with Julio in the headquarters, while Junuz went into action with the other part of the unit. Judging by the secrecy, and by the fact that Mrs. Flintstone didn't know about the strictly conf. date and time of the action, it was something big and serious. Davor was frightened, tired, short of sleep. They were talking about deblockading (unstrangleholding) Sarajevo. All units were to attack on all fronts simultaneously. The Chetniks would be surprised and unable to respond with their artillery. When the stranglehold was broken, and that would be done by the so-called assault groups, Mirza and people like him would be followed by Davor and people like him, to take the wounded prisoner and stabilize the new lines of defense. (I hope I have inserted the technical terms in the appropriate places.) Davor shook his head, he didn't believe it was possible, he kept repeating that they had a well-armed and trained army against them, and one that had been convinced that it was defending its homes and hearths. (If the media were to be believed, in B&H one percent of the citizens had cookers, all the others used hearths!)

However, it seems that the action had been abandoned.

In the afternoon Julio brought a courier with a message: Davor was to get ready at once for a long stay in the field and to report immediately to the day-nursery. A little later Julio explained to us that they hadn't given up the idea of deblockading the city after all. Davor got ready. He whispered something with Sanja. From the few words I could hear I gathered that they were talking about the urgent need for them to leave Sarajevo. No matter how. Because Davor couldn't stand this any longer. After we had seen him off, Sanja took Julio to her room. Julio was ready to help. There was a way. They'd have to pay. Julio knew who. He had acquaintances in Unprofor, he knew the Serbian officer to contact, and he also knew our lads on the barricades by the airport. He'd have to pay for press-cards as well. They were, in fact, plane tickets.

What did all that cost?

They'd discuss it.

Davor came back in the evening, adorned with military contraptions and props like a mannequin in the window of a weapons shop. They had waited in the day-nursery all day. No one knew or said anything. Junuz had let him go, because of his expectant wife. But if anything happened, a courier would come for him.

Sanja was cheerful, she made millyfoil tea, then the two of them would go to beddybies, she had washed and ironed their jim-jams, the roomlet smelled all minty. Davor was confused. He was glad that his superiors had grasped that they couldn't charge through a brick wall, but at the same time he was put out that his superiors were after all capable of grasping such a thing. When I went into their room half an hour later, to tell Davor that the courier had come for him, he was already in his pajamas.

We listened the whole night, but heard neither gunfire nor crashing shells, just from time to time the Serbs would fire a rocket flare and for a few seconds artificial moonlight would hover over the city. It seemed that the production The Liberation of Sarajevo had been postponed yet again. But in the morning Fata came in a state of great anxiety. She was puffing so hard that the cobwebs in the display cases vibrated. Her Junuz had been thrown back. (Therefore, Davor had been thrown back with him. The expression was a new military term. It denoted a fighter or group which had nothing to attack with, nor anywhere to retreat to.)

What happened?

They went last night. On the road. There was no guide, and they went behind the Chetniks' backs. No one knew where they were. Either captured, or killed.

We didn't hear any firing, we consoled her and ourselves.

It's behind the hills. And a Chetnik will use a cudgel as well. Just let it not be as God wills. She was going to the headquarters now, to see what was going on.

Sanja sat with her palms together pressed between her joined knees. Mother asked the *I Ching* when Davor would come back. The answer was LI. Flaming beauty. Righteous persistence brings rewards. Success. Rearing cows—happiness. All in all, the Book predicted success. Even when one peered deeper into the future, the lines of change said: Progress. The powerful prince receives regal honors in the form of fabulous horses, while the king receives him three times in the course of one day.

Julio: He had just come to let us know, he had been in the other group, he had seen Junuz pass by with his. Along the road. Those were their orders. The other groups had the same orders as well, but their commanders thought that the others wouldn't set off, so they had declined. Only Junuz had done what they agreed.

So did he know what had happened to them?

No one had heard any firing. It's true that it was behind the hills, but one of them would have managed to fire a round. There were thirteen of them. Now he had to go. He had just come to let us know. Maybe they'd go to look for them tonight.

Keep in the shade, not to be betrayed, called Brkić. While he listened to Julio, he had chewed his mustache, standing by the door, with a cup of tea in one hand, and a bent cigarette in the other.

Dad had discovered something as well: Junuz had deserted. That's why they hadn't fired at them. They had known they were coming. But this was a secret. Because of the morale of our fighters. Julio would go to check it out. He didn't come back for a long time. Then he reappeared: He had taken a long time, because he hadn't found anyone at headquarters. A woman had brought an unexploded shell. It had fallen through her roof and ceiling into her bed. When she came through the door with a shell in her hand, everyone in the headquarters had leapt out of the windows. But I'll let Julio tell it himself.

The Grenyade

They summons me to the headquarters, urgently. I gets there, and they're all crouching round the day-nursery and peering from behind Golfs. What's happened, some woman has brought a grenyade, it had dropped into her dough and hadn't exploded. I goes in to dismantle it, thinking of what they told us on the course, that there's no more dangerous grenyade than an unexploded one. In one they'd sent a packet of condoms packed into it. By the time security discovered that they had little holes in the top, half the medical personnel were expecting. Another grenyade fell full of raw coffee. The headquarters was decimated until it was decided whose wife would roast it and whose would grind it. A third was filled with spectacles for the blind, we sold that to the police, they now have spectacles like they used to have caps. I slowly turns the lighter, there's no flint, that's why it hadn't activated. Inside is a plastic bag, in the bag matchboxes, in the boxes tobacco. I rolls one, lights it, I haven't even had three puffs, and through the smoke I see: Bosnia free, green with grass as though covered with a carpet, sheep grazing everywhere, and kangaroos bounding. I asks my superior if I can give them back some of their own medicine. How? So and so? OK, only I'll have to wrap it in something, so it doesn't break. I takes off my beret, wraps it up, shoves everything into the grenyade, climbs up to the top of the building, watches where I can throw it so it lands in something soft and doesn't break. I chooses a puddle, takes aim, only just as I throw it, a great sow surfaces from the mud and the grenyade makes straight for her. The sow tips onto her back like a fish and the grenyade jumps away onto dry land. Their engineer rushes straight up. Opens the grenyade, takes out the beret, and when he sees what I've wrapped in it, he keels over like a post. Up comes a nurse, shakes him, puts a little bottle of brine under his nose, he doesn't budge. She takes a bottle of alcohol out of her bag, suckles him with that, again nothing. Her heart breaks. She starts wailing, a slender green pine and he goes and dries up, poor thing. And she tears the sock from her head and pulls the fastenings from her bulletproof vest and takes a drag from that bottle of alcohol. Just then the engineer comes to, but when he sees the empty bottle he too starts wailing, until both of them collapse into the quagmire. Help arrives. Four men run up with a stretcher, while a fifth drives them on with a pistol. The four of them run straight into the quagmire, haul the sow onto the stretcher and go back. And the lieutenant stands and looks at what I put in the beret. And keeps rubbing his head with his hand, as though he can't find his face with so much hair and thick beard. In the end he takes out his knife to cut his hair and shave, but his hand turns of its own accord out of habit and he cuts his own throat. Now no one else dares to come. They send a pigeon with a message to say they need tangks. But when it gets up in the air, it turns once round itself and comes over to our side. And on the way it relieves itself, and out of the whole command chooses the chaplain. The priest is downcast, he sees that God is reprimanding him. He takes off his robe, and in his leather coat walks straight into the quagmire. He takes the beret out of the mud and out of the beret my mirror. At that moment the sun comes out and the mirror flashes and blinds the priest. And he takes out his cross, and following it like a compass makes straight from the quagmire to the command. And after him go a hundred and one piglets.

Mrs. Flintstone is in despair. They say that her Junuz has gone over to the Chetniks. But whoever knows Junuz knows that that is simply not possible. She had once heard him in his sleep planning to go over to the Chetniks, and when they had had too much to eat and drink, he'd take them all prisoner and drive them back: both the Chetniks and their heavy guns.

Julio had fresh news: It seemed that it was all part of a plan. Our men gave themselves up, in order to attract attention to the wrong side of town, the main deblockade would be on the other side. Although no one had asked him anything, he whispered to me in passing that Mirza was with Davor, too.

But on the other hand Dad had discovered that our men weren't up there at all. Junuz's army had scattered before the action, and he had hastily dreamed this up.

We are entering night. Mother is counting yarrow twigs, I'm playing patience, we are waiting for news. Then we imagine the worst, and want no longer to hear anything new. Sanja is in her room. In the afternoon she took a tranquilizer, had a sleep, and now she's trying not to wake up too much. She's smoking a lot, one after the other. Brkić is beside her, rolling cigarettes, for himself and for her. Although his hands tremble, and he keeps coughing, not a trace of tobacco falls outside the paper.

At midnight Julio woke us. We were all in the kitchen, dressed, sleeping in our chairs, as we had each given ourselves up to our thoughts and schemes. Our men had come back! Davor, too! They were in the headquarters, writing a report. How they had gone, where they had been, what they did, who they saw. They wouldn't be back before morning.

At last we can go to bed.

I was the first to leap at Davor and give him a hug. Only later did I count all his arms and legs and establish that everything was in its right place and quantity. He only had a few scratches and bruises as a result of last night's race.

When they had discovered that they had crossed into Serbian territory, behind their own front lines, they had spent the night and the following day in the cellar of a house, and at dusk made their way back. They were spotted when they were right near a stream, so they ran through the gorge, down waterfalls and over rocks, and so got away. No one was wounded, their only loss was a box full of ammunition, which they had dropped, because it was heavy. Mirza had gone back for it first thing this morning.

And was there any news?

Of the box or Mirza?

I deserved that, since no one held my tongue. You shouldn't ask anything. Everything would happen the way it was destined to, regardless of whether we knew that or not.

I had told myself that I would finish the story about the lodgers when our number or composition changed, or when they finally relocated us, together with the exhibits. Although something like that had happened nearly a month ago, it was only today that I had gathered enough time and willpower finally to do it. I am still wondering how it could all have happened in one day. Virtually in one afternoon.

I hope I'll have the heart and will to describe it.

It began the day before, with Julio putting down the telephone receiver. Tomorrow, he had said. Davor had to be in the park at seven. An Unprofor transporter would come for them. It would take them to the airport. Then Zagreb and Frankfurt.

Davor was on edge. He had got ready, waited for the call, and when the journey had at last been confirmed, he was having second thoughts: He couldn't leave his expectant wife just before the birth.

His expectant wife just before the birth looked at him, then tried to convince him: He couldn't help her. It would be easier for her without him. As soon as the baby was strong enough, she'd follow him.

Julio was getting irritated: In two months time the people in Unprofor would change, it would be more expensive, if it were possible at all. And who knows where he himself would be. The army was the army. He wouldn't be guarding a barricade in the middle of town forever.

Mother said that psychic stability was the most important thing. If Davor left, Sanja would be calm, and then the birth would happen without any problems.

Sanja was in her element, the center of attention, brave, selfless, once again prepared to carry a burden she could not even pick up: He had to be realistic. They couldn't leave town together. And it was stupid to stay. They had given all the money they had for the little blue card.

The conversation was interrupted when Brkić came in. He was the only one not to approve. His observations pounced on Davor like a fox on a henhouse: Why was it stupid to stay?

Because there was no life here anymore. Their friends were leaving. Wild, coarse people were moving in. There was no future. There was no work. This was a dead city. They were young, they could succeed. There was no happiness here.

And where was there?

In Australia.

Whoever runs away once, spends his whole life running. If you're not a Gypsy, don't live like a Gypsy. They were born here.

Bullets hissed. Shrapnel. Shells. And there was no end to it. Winter was coming.

They were not the only ones. Nor was this the first war.

It was the first for them.

That's why it seemed more terrible than it was.

And it was brutal. Blood, ruins, firing, cries, funerals on foggy mornings and at gloomy dusks. We had no friends left, no homes, no things that greeted us every morning to confirm that we were still here. Dolls, serviettes, a globe, photographs, books, records, drawings, letters, wastepaper baskets, hangers, pillows, they were all just things. They could be collected again. The same or different, better or worse, they could be got back. They could be looked for.

But what about loves packed into envelopes without a stamp, what about days transformed into twilights, what, in the end, about all those babies who had stayed or been taken away to grow up without their fathers, grannies, and granddads? The first smile, tooth, word, that could not be looked for, or made up for. I think this was the kind of thing that Davor may have been thinking about on that last day and this was what he didn't talk about with Sanja. Brkić put it more briefly: Credit for cash.

He, too, had prepared his rucksack, from that former war, and his spoon, on the handle of which he had made a gismo, and now he carried it in his pocket like a fountain pen. (Gismo is the common name for all small but useful and practical inventions, which are sufficiently insignificant not to have their own names.)

Dad would not surrender. He had succeeded in postponing the eviction, but they could come again any day. He was looking for new space for the museum. They told him not to hurry, there was a war on. He asked who it was then who was in a hurry to move the museum. It was wartime for all of us. Dad says that there are two authorities in the city. One is official, civic, and has no power over anyone, it isn't in a position even to protect a rotten tree in a park from being cut down. This is the one people curse when things go wrong. The other authority is secret. The Party. It doesn't meet during the day, or in public places. This is the one that decides the fates of people. And the museum.

Julio had let Davor and Sanja have his accumulator. There was light in their room. Their things were packed. They had been already because of the threatened eviction. I went in several times, and always found the same scene. Sanja was busy over little things, pushing them into the bag, which Davor later took them out of, because she would need them. Hard currency, letters, cassettes of his documentary dramas . . .
   Sniffy was lying on the floor, with his nose between his front feet. He did not take his eyes off Davor. Whenever Davor looked at him, he wagged his tail and raised his head. But Davor didn't have time to play with him. He didn't have the strength either. He could at least have said goodbye to him.

From there I went to Brkić. He was leaving at dawn as well. I hope that he will give me something when we part. At least a proverb. Like this one: If you hit the center, you've missed everything else. But the old Sioux did not kiss me, did not offer me a last cigarette, did not leave me his battered copy of *How the Steel Was Tempered,* with a dedication on the first page. But maybe he did after all: the lesson that those to whom you give most, give back the least. Like me with Mother.

The last image: he's lying, covered in a horse blanket, with his rucksack under his head and a towel over the rucksack, his hands on his stomach. He can't sleep, but he's pretending, he can't breathe, but he's trying. Beside the bed are his so-called HTP-shoes (Hygiene, Technology, Protection) and in them woolen socks. On the table an ashtray, greasy cards, a newspaper, and on the newspaper, multicolored gloves. A present from Sanja. I admit, I'm jealous.

Good night, Leader.

In the morning of that last day of my story, I hurried to Julio, to snatch a hot drink and details about Brkić's departure. I found him standing over a pan of camomile tea, which he was trying to drink with his nose. Mother was encouraging him. Wrapped in towels, he was speaking softly, as though at his last gasp: Flu. Influenza. An insidious disease. It attacks a person at the worst possible time. Him for instance. Who would go with Davor now?

Mother was smiling: There's no need to pretend.

He wasn't pretending. He was covered in sweat, his throat was swollen.

It was about Granny's little suitcase, wasn't it? If Mother gave it to Julio, he would get better immediately and he'd be able to go with Davor?

He wasn't thinking of the suitcase. He had lost the bet. Brkić had gone and now it didn't matter.

Sanja came in: Did Mother have anything they could use to make Davor sandwiches to take with him? Mother said perhaps it wouldn't be necessary. Julio was ill, so Davor couldn't go either, because Julio was the only one who knew the Serbian officer for the contact with Unprofor, who were Davor's only guarantee that on the way to the airfield (havocfield), the Serbian customs men would not pluck him out of the transporter like a strawberry out of cream.

I stood and watched, finally everything was clear to me. I had before me the theme of a classical tragedy. No one wanted Davor to leave, but everyone was doing all they could to help him go, because they believed it would be better for him to leave. While he, although he didn't want to go, was leaving because it would be easiest for everyone.

Julio wasn't the only one. Brkić also knew the officer.

Yes, but Brkić had left.

No he hadn't. Sanja had asked him to stay.

Julio's nose finally took in a good mouthful, but I didn't have time to see whether he would get by without artificial breathing apparatus. I went back with Sanja to her room, in which Brkić and Davor were just finishing a showdown over a game of preference. (Preference is a game with thirty-two cards, for three players, in which the aim is that two get together and hammer the third. It's very like this war, in that way.)

Dad came before lunch. He was not alone. Three other members of the resistance movement with French berets and pruned beards passed through the museum with him. Then Dad stayed to smoke a cigarette, while the commission continued its circuit alone. We had just reached the crucial moment, and we didn't get up to say good-bye. Their presence reminded me of the first days of the uprising, when snipers were sought even behind the pictures on the walls.

One proposed that this should be the accounts department.

Another was calculating the floor space.

The third thought that the student affairs office would be more suitable. The room didn't get the sun, but the parquet and window panes had been preserved. There was a chimney as well.

The second looked at his watch. He'd be late for lunch.

The first looked at the table with the cards, the way I, I imagine, looked at Sniffy on his streetwalker. He made a note of something, probably that the table would have to be specially disinfected. Maybe the whole room as well. Cards were the devil's work.

The second frowned and shook his head when I drew out a solo ace, and walked out demonstratively when I played it. *Domini canes,* muttered Dad, coming back after he had seen them out. Literally translated, the phrase meant dogs of faith, but it meant keepers of the faith.

Mrs. Flintstone, who was drawn to anxiety like a bee to a flower, buzzed through the museum looking for somewhere to insert her proboscis. Fortunately, the rest of us, in the expectation of the planned eviction, were packing our things in bundles and suitcases, so Davor's didn't look suspicious among them. He was sitting in the kitchen, calmer than the rest of us, writing his will, as he called his list for managing Sniffy in a sour wisecrack. He was trying to conceal his shame and unease with jokes. That dog, which was shoving its nose into his lap, had been and remained the only real reason for them to stay: not patriotism, not his job, not the family, and not even the risky pregnancy, had been sufficiently firm motives to keep them here. It was only Sniffy. In him everything had become wound up and entangled: love with fear, respect with calculation, devotion with vanity.

Some people came and took away packing cases containing exhibits. Julio pretended to help them, while Dad tried to get in their way. In passing, miserably, he said that they had taken down the large iron and copper letters above the museum entrance, they had pulled them out of the wall and left holes in the plaster, as though from Chetnik shrapnel. He had heard that they were planning to concrete over the cobbles in the hall where the model was. The stones for those cobbles, said Dad, were taken out of the Drina River a hundred years ago. Each stone, white and round, had been weighed and stroked by the architect in person. Dad was talking incoherently. Having lost the war, he was now losing the battle as well.

At two o'clock, Davor and Brkić weren't there. They had left earlier, said Sanja, because Brkić, sick and exhausted by so much lying down, needed more time. But I think that they left in a hurry so that Davor would not change his mind or cry. He slipped out of this episode of his life like a thief. The war, despite Sanja and Sniffy, or Mother and me, had made Davor's life into an infinite desert, in which, tormented by barren shame, malevolent fear, and burning desires, instead of salvation and escape, he sought only a slightly nicer fata morgana.

And therefore, when Mirza began to praise Davor's courage and sangfroid, in that outing behind the Chetnik lines, I saw this friendship-manqué crumbling to dust at the very first embrace, like a dried-up mummy. It was an early autumn afternoon, one of those in which the sun succeeds only with difficulty in warming the white stone steps. Mirza and I were sitting in the museum park and watching Sniffy snorting and snuffling through the little piles of fallen leaves. I was wearing my earring, the golden knight with his large raised hand, and waiting for that to be noticed. And then!

A short, sharp whistle. Mirza pushing me onto the ground and lying on top of me. An explosion of which I heard nothing, apart from a hissing in my ears. Over us and around us fell pieces of beam, brick, tiles, branches, glass. Dad rushed up and dragged me into the museum. Mirza shook lumps of earth and pine needles out of his hair and collar. In the dark corridor Mother and Sanja were waiting for us. Mother was holding a spoon and a kitchen cloth in her hands, Sanja Chekhov: Had Sniffy been with us?

Mirza said he had, and wanted to go out again. Dad was against it: It wasn't sensible. Shells never fall singly. There are always at least two. Mirza opened the door nevertheless, and in the doorway, as in the frame of a painting, we saw the broken iron railings and under them, white in the red leaves, Sniffy. Sanja stood, white as chalk, pursed blue lips, trembling. Mother hugged her, to calm and warm her. Outside Mirza was kneeling beside Sniffy and bandaging him. A good sign. That was his magic bandage, the one of which it was written that it would save someone's life. His hands were red. And as he carried him between us, through the dark, narrow corridor, as through a tunnel, the only thing that shone were Sniffy's eyes and the blood on his white hide.

Sanja wanted to go with him. Dad wouldn't hear of it: Mirza could drive, he knew where he could find a car, he knew where the vet was. There was no need for us all to expose ourselves. If some-one had to, then he would. In the end we sat down at the table, as though having lunch. But no one ate anything. Mother gave up coaxing us, she moved to one end of the couch and sat in the lotus position. A second later she was already on the path following Putaparta. Sanja read the instructions for managing Sniffy. At least half-an-hour's walk a day. If there was shelling, then in the museum park. No sugar on any account. Clean his teeth once a week.

The shells were falling—one minute nearby, the next further away, as though a drunken bearded god was tap-dancing over the city. We heard pieces of other people's roofs crashing over our tiles.

Dad was smoking and didn't see that the ash was falling onto the food in his plate. Sanja said something. She seemed calm, but her voice trembled. She said something that I didn't understand at first. Dad and Julio went out at once, and Mother pulled the handle on her flying couch. Then I realized what she had said: The Waters. Had broken.

I ran over all the lessons I had collected from several books about pregnancy and birth. However I looked at it, the breaking of the waters was the beginning of labor.

Mother held Sanja's hand: She shouldn't worry. It would all be fine. Dad and Julio would bring a car in a few minutes. Had she packed her things for the hospital?

Yes. They were in the case. No, Davor took the case. In a plastic bag.

I brought her the plastic bag. She asked for shoes.

But the car intended for this purpose was not at the headquarters. Mirza had used it to take Sniffy. Mrs. Junuz-bey offered the keys of their Golf. Dad tried to turn on the engine, but nothing happened. We pushed, leaned all our weight against it, groaned, as though it was us who were giving birth. A first attempt, a second, a third. Nothing. Little pieces of tile fell into the gutters above us. Julio rocked the dead horse. (The similarity between a car and medicine is not only that they are now rare, but that before use they have to be stirred.) There was gas in the tank. The spark-plugs were all right. Fata thought that her Junuz had jumbled the wires: He would bend down under the steering wheel and fiddle with something there, so there was no way anyone could steal it. Julio and Dad then checked the wires.

Sanja couldn't stand up. Her face was contorted. She was completely stiff, bent to one side. Mother was holding her hand. I was standing beside them. I was holding a towel, but I didn't know what to do with it. I was holding a glass of water as well, I didn't know what to do with that, either. The contractions were getting more frequent. Sanja's last labor had come soon and gone quickly as well. That speed was why the baby hadn't survived. Then it was peacetime, it happened in the hospital, and shells weren't clanging all around. Mother was beside her, stroking her and repeating *om, om, om.* (This was not a resistance unit, but the sound out of which, according to one Eastern belief, the universe sprang. When a person repeats that sound, as Mother was doing, all the good spirits come to drive away the evil ones, positive energy to deflect negative.) Dad, upset and betrayed, caught off-guard and helpless, informed us that, despite all their efforts, they had not succeeded in turning the engine, and that Julio had gone to the headquarters, to create another vehicle, and to telephone Pete Bringforth. Mother shook her head, so that Sanja didn't see. The door opened and the woman I had poked fun at and in my spoiled manner called Mrs. Flintstone let someone through in front of her, introducing him as a neighbor, a doctor, a gynecologist.

The water was boiling, clean towels were prepared. Dad and I were superfluous and we went out into the atrium. For a few moments the splinters of glass in the windows were still as brilliant as lead, and then one after the other they were extinguished and the first shadows of twilight fell. The thunder of the heavy artillery and detonations was stilled. They're cooling the barrels, said Dad. In that almost festive silence we sometimes heard Sanja's muffled cry, which slipped out from under her promise to herself that she would not scream and wail.

Julio returned with Mirza. Sniffy had stayed. Forever. Mirza had waited, although they had told him there was no hope. They gave him an injection. The dog was calm, he trembled a few times and tried to raise his head. Mirza thought he was looking for Davor.

We stayed sitting outside, although the walls were losing their warmth and becoming increasingly cold. Mirza wrapped his windbreaker around me but my teeth went on chattering. None of us had the courage to go in and see what was going on, and it didn't occur to them inside to come and tell us that there was no reason to worry. Dad had dragged a wooden cradle out of one of his hidden recesses and was wiping the dust off it with a handkerchief. The cradle was a hundred years old, carved, with two embossed six-pointed stars on its round sides. Julio was crouching, leaning against the doorpost. It is strange how old people, when they are thoughtful or dozing, look smaller than they really are. As though something came out of them and wandered off down the leaf-covered cobbles. I had never before seen him for so long in one place. The cold made the little flame in the glass with the gold monogram flicker. Through the glass lace on the edges the flourish of light blinked over the wall. I walked about, sat down and stood up, fiddled with my extravagant candle, and drove my evil forebodings back into the blackness out of which they had assaulted me once again. I told myself that Sniffy had sacrificed himself so that everything would be all right with the baby. Then it occurred to me that misfortunes don't come singly. And what had happened to Sanja two years ago, I now saw and understood as though it had happened to me. She was lying a few rooms away from the room with the incubators. She didn't know what to do with her breasts out of which the milk had started to drip and hurt her. The baby's condition was worsening. Sanja read Chekhov, the same short stories several times. She wept ceaselessly. The other women cursed her, angry that her tears and snivelling would make their milk dry up. A woman doctor came and took her to see the baby. The little being was lying on its side, in a little glass box, with tubes in its nose, with plasters on its hand and chest, with long tousled black hair. She was the largest and most beautiful baby in the room. She died half-an-hour later. From injuries sustained during the birth.

And now perhaps it was all happening again, we knew it all and had been through it all, nothing could surprise us, but again we were secondary and helpless. Why couldn't we hear anything? Why didn't anyone come? Why didn't Dad or Julio go to ask? If the wick went out in the wind, it would not be good. If there were a shooting star, it would be OK. If there were more than two hundred paving stones on the ground, it would be. If I blinked, it would not be. If between four drainpipes I managed to see the whole of the Plough, it would succeed. If I didn't stop casting spells and incantations, I would open my eyes and see myself in splinters of glass, knocking on wood, shifting from my place and repeating, like a mechanical doll: *inshallah, om,* godwilling. The greater the desert fear creates in us, the more powerfully sacred words echo in our emptiness. Or was that the bell over the entrance to the museum?

Someone opened the door, two shapes came into the atrium, in one of them we recognized Junuz. The other silhouette was smaller, bent, dragging its feet as it walked. Junuz was supporting it with one hand, and in the other carrying, as will very soon be revealed,

Granny's suitcase. Junuz evidently found his companion heavy, and he set him down carefully by the wall of the well. Only then did we recognize Brkić. He was wheezing, his cap had fallen over his eyes, his beard onto his chest. He tried to straighten up, grabbed Granny's suitcase, and knocked it into the well. Julio leapt up, but was too late. The suitcase splashed into the mud at the bottom. Junuz and Dad undid Brkić's coat. Julio asked for more light, struck his flint lighter, stared over the wall into the well. Dad took off his own jacket, folded it and placed it under Brkić's head. But Julio pushed him away and laid Brkić's head in his lap: Old man, old man! It's me. I didn't fly after the suitcase. You don't have to fuck around anymore. Boško . . . hey, Boško . . .

His hand was shaking, the wick bent over, darkness poured over the atrium, in which, suddenly, neither gasping nor breathing could be heard. Out of that silence, which lasted a moment, but seemed like eternity, a scene from Brkić's recollections of his village leapt up before me, the village he had left as a teenager and to which he had never returned. The village: a hundred white houses, on the banks of two rivers as on two calloused, furrowed palms. A cicada in a quarry, sun on a waterfall between poplars. A small, fragrant apricot tree on the boundary of a vineyard, a snakeskin on an acacia thorn. A red roof through the leaves of a mulberry, a well under a walnut tree, doves on the chimney, red peppers drying under the eaves. A high threshold, a beaten earth floor, an open window, a wooden sword eaten away by the juice of knocked off burdock heads. On the hill above two rivers, in the middle of four oak trees, a graveyard.

In the dark, someone began to whistle: Down with force and injustice . . .

I lit the wick. Julio was staring into the face in front of him, Dad had already grasped what Junuz had known from the beginning. Brkić grinned, then straightened up, took off his cap, pulled off his false beard, and I heard myself shout: Davor!

Then Julio got up, bent over the well, then turned and looked again: Was that the right suitcase?

Yes.

Empty?

Full. Brkić had sent it to Julio, to look after.

But they were interrupted by a scream from inside. Davor under-stood everything in a flash. She's in labor, said Dad, but Davor didn't hear him. He was already running inside.

Behind the door, Junuz took out the Shakespeare and began in silence to wind a string, which rose off the ground and was seen to lead to the well. Julio snatched the stick from him and continued turning the little machine, as though he were fishing in the well. The suitcase banged against the walls a few times, and then, covered in mud, appeared over the edge of the wall.

From the room came the weak cry of a baby.

Julio opened the suitcase.

Our neighbor came with a candle: A little girl, *mashallah!*

Julio opened the suitcase. He was excited and he dropped it twice. Inside he found a bundle of white cotton materials and lace. He unwrapped them. They were empty. He felt them again, but this time more slowly and carefully. Still nothing came out. Then he realized what he was holding in his hands: baby clothes. I recog-nized them as well. They had dressed my Granny, Mother, and me. And now they would clothe the little princess. Godwilling.

■ □ ■ □ ■

ABOUT THE AUTHOR

Nenad Veličković was born in 1962. The author of numerous television scripts and radio plays as well as novels and short stories, he lives in Sarajevo. From 1992 to 1996 he served in the army of Bosnia-Herzegovina.

■ □ ■ □ ■

WRITINGS FROM AN UNBOUND EUROPE

For a complete list of titles, see the Writings from an Unbound Europe Web site at www.nupress.northwestern.edu/ue.